Phil Redmond's

LUKE'S
secret diary

Also available from Channel 4 Books

Hollyoaks: The Lives and Loves of Finn

Phil Redmond's

HOLLYOAKS
A MERSEY TELEVISION COMPANY

LUKE'S
secret diary

KADDY BENYON

First published 2001 by Channel 4 Books
an imprint of Pan Macmillan Ltd
Pan Macmillan, 20 New Wharf Road, London N1 9RR
Basingstoke and Oxford
Associated companies throughout the world
www.panmacmillan.com

ISBN 0 752 27210 1

13 15 17 19 18 16 14 12

A CIP catalogue record for this book is available from
the British Library.

Photographs © The Mersey Television Company Limited
Typeset by Blackjacks
Printed and bound by Mackays of Chatham plc, Chatham, Kent

This book accompanies the television series *Hollyoaks* made by
The Mersey Television Company for Channel 4.
Series Producer: Jo Hallows
Executive Producer: Phil Redmond

I was on top form last night. I went into town with a few lads from school to celebrate the end of term and ended up pulling three girls, one of them from right under Jez's nose. The first one was this girl Alison who I had a bit of a thing with over Christmas. She was with her new boyfriend, but she made it very clear she still fancied me, so I said I'd follow her outside in five minutes. Alison's a babe and she's got a lovely pair, but she's a bit uptight. We stopped seeing each other when she caught me getting off with her little sister at her house. I still think dumping me was a bit harsh. How was I to know I was snogging the wrong sister? They look really alike and it was dark. Anyway, she told me she'd missed me, and was just in the middle of showing me how much, when her boyfriend came out looking for her. Bad timing. I left them to yell at each other and went back inside for a few more drinks with the others. Then Jez finally scored with this girl he'd spent all evening chatting up – I didn't catch her name. Things started to look a bit ropey when they started chewing each other's faces off right in front of me. So I went for a wander and that's when I spotted Amy. She's Jez's ex from hell, every time I see her I hear the *Psycho* music. They broke up last summer and she will not leave him alone, she always wants to 'talk'. She started having a go at him and he eventually agreed to go out to the beer garden and 'talk' with her, leaving me to look after his bird. So I did, and he's majorly hacked off with me. I was only being friendly! We had to walk home cos it was so late, on the way we saw Lara Jacobs and her mates from the upper sixth eating chips. I really fancy Lara, so I decided to be cheeky and asked her if I could have one – a chip wasn't all I got! That puts the current 1999 score sheet at Me:15 and Jez:11 – he's no competition for Morgan and his organ!

Sunday 28 March 1999 – 11:57pm

I am so bored. Dad reckons I should get a job or something, then I wouldn't have time to be bored, but there's no way I'm slaving my guts out in my holidays, not until I have to. Beth's got Mum and Dad so wrapped around her little finger getting them to pay for her skiing trip. And just before her GCSEs as well. I mean she promised to take some revision with her but come on, she'll be far too busy getting trolleyed with her mates and flirting with ski instructors. Oh well, she was never going to get any As anyway. Adam's got an alright number though, he's working as a lifeguard at the college pool. He reckons there's some great totty down there, he says his boss, Jas, is really tasty. Might have to go and check her out for myself, if things don't liven up around here.

Monday 29 March 1999 – 7:28pm

Things are definitely looking up. I got Adam to blag me a free pass to his gym yesterday and he was right, seriously nice totty. I saw that Jas bird he keeps going on about, she's alright, but nothing special – a bit too tomboyish for me. She had a gorgeous friend though, called Ruth, and she's older, well, not geriatric or anything, but older than me, a final year student at HCC. She's got the sexiest eyes, you know the kind that say 'right here, right now', makes me horny just thinking about it. And you know what they say about older women – years of experience and all that. I saw her checking me out when I got in the pool, couldn't keep her eyes off me. I'd have asked her to come in and join me, but she's got a broken leg. I made sure she saw me giving her the eye and I gave her my best puppy dog look. It's always a winner that one. Even though she was yakking away to Jas, she kept looking at me to see if I was looking at her. I made sure I bumped into her on my way out. I thought I'd missed my chance for a while, though, cos she was talking to some short lad – turns out he was her step-brother or something. We had a coffee and I asked her if she wanted to go out some time, but she said her life was 'Complicated', whatever that means. I wrote my number down and told her to call me. She acted like she wouldn't but I knew she would, and she did, about ten minutes ago. We're going out next week. Ster-ike!

Thursday 1 April 1999 – 6:55am

Morgan shoots… and he scores! Sometimes I surprise even myself with my pulling powers. I have just got in from spending the night with Ruth, didn't take me long to win her over, did it? We met up at a bar in town for a few drinks, she looked really sexy, in a low-cut black dress. We had a bit of a chat and got to know each other – turns out her dad owns The Dog in The Pond, which is our local. It's a bit of a dive, but it's okay if you don't want to go into town. She told me she'd dreamt about me the night before and that was when I knew I was in. I suppose I should have been a bit intimidated, what with her being older and more experienced, but I reckon I'm pretty advanced for my age. I tried to get her to tell me the details of the dream, but she just went red and changed the subject, I bet it was horny. Wha-hey! I was about to hit her with a line about how I've been known to make girls' dreams come true, but she got me flummoxed by asking me if I'm a student. I nearly blew my cover – she'd freak if she knew I'm only seventeen. I told her I'd just come back from travelling in Australia for my gap year. Good bit of quick thinking there, Morgan. Anyway, now for the best bit, we got to the end of the night and we were getting on really well. Before I had a chance to make my move she invited me back for 'coffee' – and we all know what that means. The funny thing is, she was the one who jumped on me. That's older women for you. We didn't hang about, either – we ended up doing it everywhere, in the lounge, kitchen, bathroom – we would have done it in the bath if her leg wasn't still in plaster. It wasn't a hindrance, though, we just had to be a bit creative with positions, if you know what I mean! It's definitely true about older women being more experienced. Being with Ruth was an education, alright. Younger girls are always so nervous and uptight. With a girl like Ruth you can tell she knows exactly what she wants. I'm pretty sure I came up to scratch – I didn't get any complaints – though there were a few little awkward bits. Still, you know what they say, 'practice makes perfect'. I'm completely knackered though – we finally went to bed at about four. I couldn't sleep, though, cos I'm not used to sharing my bed for longer than an hour or so. I left her a note and came back here. Mum and Dad gave me a right ear-bashing for staying out all night and not telling them. I told them I was at Jez's working on a physics project and, can you believe, they fell for it! Suckers.

2:31pm

I've only just woken up. Mum and Dad wanted me to come and look at the site they've just bought for their bistro, but I couldn't be bothered. They took Zara with them which is good, cos now I have the whole house to myself and I don't have to listen to her squawking to her boy-band CDs. I got a postcard from Jeremy, he reckons he's got to third base with a girl in France. Just wait till I tell him about Ruth, man is he going to be jealous?! An older woman – and a fit one at that. Yes, I've surpassed myself this time.

Friday 2 April 1999 – 11:55pm

Dad's doing his nut. Someone crashed a car into the new bistro last night and the place is wrecked. Maybe this'll make him see it was a bad idea from the start. I mean, it was hardly a prime location, next to a video shop and opposite some junk yard. What kind of people would eat somewhere round there anyway? If he ever bothered to ask my opinion, maybe he wouldn't end up making such a mess of things. I just heard Adam come in, I bet he's been with that Jas again. Personally, I don't know why he's still hanging around with her, he got what he wanted ages ago. He always lets women get their claws into him. I want to tell him about me and Ruth, he'd be so impressed, but she made me promise not to tell cos of her boyfriend finding out. Girls just don't understand that half the fun of getting it on with them, is to tell your mates about it afterwards.

Easter Sunday 4 April 1999 – 10:23pm

Everyone's downstairs watching a stupid film. I'm really bored. I tried to ring Ruth to see if she wanted to do something, but she was out. I only got two Easter eggs this year, I used to get loads when I was a kid.

Easter Monday 5 April 1999 – 9:36pm

What a nightmare, I've been totally busted with Ruth. Wish I'd never got out of bed today, I hate bank holidays. Mum and Dad always make us go out for family meals. Total snore. We got dragged along to The Dog today – well Zara didn't, she made herself sick after eating all her Easter eggs in the night. I didn't really want to go to the Dog with Mum and Dad cos I knew Ruth would be there helping her Dad out. It hardly boosts your shaggability, going drinking with the wrinklies, does it? Ruth was really pleased to see me at first. She looked fantastic in this tight little red number. Even with the oldsters sitting there I reckoned I could get her round the back for a quick snog at least. I was giving her some chat and flirting like anything, when Mum came over and told her not to serve me booze cos I'm under age. Can you believe it? I mean, how embarrassing is that? I tried to explain, but Ruth was having none of it, she was really angry. I reckon I might have blown it there, or rather Mum did. Oh well, you win some, you lose some. Maybe she's into toyboys – a lot of older women are. I read somewhere that we blokes reach our sexual peak a lot earlier than women. And anyway, there's this other barmaid at The Dog called Carol. She's dead pretty but a bit mad. She wears all this sparkly stuff on her face and in her hair and talks at a hundred miles an hour. She definitely fancied me, so I might give her a go if Ruth's not into having the toyboy idea.

Sunday 11 April 1999 – 7:06pm

Adam and I just went for a drink, though not in The Dog – I'm giving that place a wide berth for a while. He asked my advice on Jas, apparently she wants to get serious with him. He can be a real sap sometimes with women. I knew this was going to happen, he always hangs around too long, he can never see the warning signs. I told him to tell her he doesn't feel ready for a serious relationship at the moment, it always works for me. As long as you say 'It's not you, it's me' to a girl when you're breaking up with her, they seem to take it okay. I nearly told him about me and Ruth, but I might just give her one last go, there's no point blowing it out of the water if there's still a chance.

Thursday 15 April 1999 – 9:44pm

I'm knackered. Me and Adam have been helping Dad get the bistro ready for opening. Don't know why he can't just pay some decorators to do it, I'll be glad to go back to school at this rate. I met Ruth's boyfriend today, he came to talk to Dad about the yard. I can't believe she wastes her time on a no-hoper like him. I mean, he and that lanky streak of sarcasm, Finn, say they do house clearances, but if you ask me they're just glorified bin men. I went down to the pool on my lunch break to see if Ruth was there. She wasn't and Jas was really off with me, not sure if it's because Adam's avoiding her or cos she just doesn't like me – it's probably because of Adam. Anyway, I finally found Ruth in the magazine office and she was mardy with me as well. She reckons she doesn't want to see me any more, but she wants me – I can tell. I might go and see her now, see what she's up to. There's no way she'll turn me away if I turn up at her place, I'll have to get the bus though, Adam's got Dad's car again. Man I wish I had my own wheels.

Friday 16 April 1999 – 12:33pm

What a way to spend the last day of the holidays. It turned out to be well worth my while going round to Ruth's last night. She wasn't that happy to see me at first, she was pretty freaked that I could have arrived when Lewis was still there. I told her not to worry, I know what I'm doing. She seemed quite flattered though, I don't think she expected to see me again after giving me the brush off – twice. I told her I never give up when there's a woman as beautiful as her involved. That clinched it, she couldn't keep her hands off me. This time I stayed all night. I pretended I was going for a waz about 11ish and phoned Mum to tell her I was staying at Jeremy's. The funniest thing happened this morning. I decided to make Ruth a cup of tea – I mean you've got to show some gratitude when an older woman's willing to sleep with you haven't you? I was in the kitchen minding my own business, when who should walk in in his boxers but Adam. He'd stayed with Jas. He was well surprised to see me there and pretty impressed when he realized why. I reckon he might be a bit jealous too, I mean, he definitely got the booby prize out of those two.

7:18pm

My spoilt little cow of a sister just got back from skiing. I'm really hacked off with her. I gave her seventy quid to get me some wrap-around Oakleys and she reckons she ran out of money and had to spend it. Yeah right, had to spend it on getting totally off her face every night. She still managed to get Mum and Dad a picture for the bistro though, she knows how to keep them sweet. She's such a creep.

13

Monday 19 April – 11:17pm

Went back to school today and Mrs Beck had a right go at me for not doing my homework. I wish she'd just get off my case, doesn't she realize there's more to life than quadratic equations? Jeremy was well impressed with my latest conquest, I mean older, married and only having the use of one leg is more than he could hope for in his wettest dreams, not to mention she's got a killer bod too. He reckoned he had a feel of the au pair over the holidays, but he's got to be making it up to make him look a stud.

Sunday 25 April 1999 – 7:17pm

Adam and I went to watch the football and then went out for a drink. He stayed with Jas last night but is getting really sick of her wanting to be with him all the time. He warned me to stay away from Ruth for a while cos she's told Lewis all about us. That's all I need at the moment – trouble from that git and his mates. What is she like? I don't get why girls have to ruin everything with the whole honesty thing. I mean, I bet Lewis was feeling a whole lot better before he knew – and Ruth, too, for that matter. Shame really – I was just getting into my stride. Oh well, it was fun while it lasted.

11:42pm

What a nightmare of an evening. Just got back from The Dog. You won't believe what happened. When we got there Tony, Lewis, Finn and the fat one with the pet rat were there too. They looked like they'd had a few and kept giving us evils. We were just ignoring them, but that made them worse. They accused us of stealing their girl-friends – it turns out Jas was going out with Tony until she dumped him for Adam. I told them they were a load of losers. Adam was really annoyed and said I'd provoked them, but they are losers, they must be if they don't know how to hold on to their women. Lewis was well up for a fight, he can be a right yob when he wants. He punched me right in the face, and that was it – I grabbed him and gave him such a belting. The next thing I know, all hell breaks loose and Tony's got Adam on the floor and it looks like he's trying to strangle him. Then Finn joins in and the next thing I know that fat one, I think he's called Wayne, is sitting on my chest. Then he farted, man it was disgusting, I thought I was going to suffocate. Luckily Ruth's dad pulled him off me or I'd have flattened him. We all got chucked out of the pub and we've been barred. I'm really hacked off about that cos they started it. Adam had to stop me really going for Lewis when we were outside. He said he isn't worth it and he's probably right. Lewis pointed at me and said 'you'll keep'. I think he was trying to scare me. Yeah right, as if.

Thursday 29 April 1999 – 10.00pm

I've only just got in from helping Dad out at the cafe. He and Mum have decided to call it Deva cos it's Roman for Chester – how naff is that? He reckons it's got to be ready for opening by next week. Don't know why he can't do some of the hard graft himself instead of getting me to do it. I hope he's going to back me up when I have to tell Mr Johnson why I haven't done my chemistry assignment. Dad went ape at me at breakfast when he saw my bruises from the fight. He didn't have a chance to have a go at Adam about his cos he was on the early shift at the pool. He reckons we've let him down and ruined his street cred around here – as if he had any in the first place. He made me go and see Ruth's dad to apologise, I hate him sometimes, he wouldn't even listen when I tried to tell him we didn't start it. It really hacks me off – he never listens to a word I have to say, just shouts orders at me the whole time like as if I was a little kid. Anyway, I went along with him just to keep the peace and who was there when I went round, but Ruth. She ignored me which really annoyed me. I mean, she's the one who was going out with someone else, she's the one who was unfaithful and yet I'm the one left feeling crap about the whole thing. Seems like I'm everybody's whipping boy round here. So I went round to see her at her flat tonight. I thought maybe now Lewis is out of the picture we could pick up where we left off. I tried my best to seduce her but she was having none of it. She gave me this spiel about not being into casual relationships – hardly the impression I got! I told her we didn't even have to have a relationship, it doesn't bother me, I'm just happy to have sex with her. That didn't wash either. She was a bit patronising actually, she said that sex with someone you have feelings for is much better than a one night stand. Oh well, her loss.

Thursday 13 May 1999 – 8:32pm

Typical isn't it? I deliberately scheduled extra football practice tonight after school so I wouldn't have to go to the grand opening of Deva and it turns out I really missed a right laugh. For starters, Jas turned up and was giving Adam a hard time cos he hasn't rung her for ages. She had a real go at him about two-timing her. He didn't have a clue what she was on about cos (a) they were never officially an item and (b) he hasn't been seeing anyone else. Then she went over to Beth and told her to watch him, he'd cheat on her, too. She only thought Beth and Adam were together! Apparently I missed a classic moment when Beth told her she was Adam's sister. I wish I'd seen her face. Adam says he's definitely going to bin her off after that. The other thing was that Wayne fell through the ceiling and landed right on Dad's wontons. He says he was trying to save his rat or something, but I reckon he was up to something pervy. Mum's been crying ever since they got home and Dad's gone mental. I'm staying out of the way, I mean, I can't help but see the funny side of a great lard-arse just falling out of the sky with a rat in his hand. That's classic, that is.

Sunday 16 May 1999 – 11:02pm

Had a nightmare weekend. Me and Jez went for a drink in The Dog – we couldn't face town cos the racing's on. I was really flirting with Carol and just when I thought it was a sure thing, she went and asked Jez for his phone number. He thinks it's hilarious – yeah, ha ha, she's too ditzy for me anyway. Mum and Dad are doing my head in, they keep arguing about Deva. Mum reckons that the Wayne incident is an omen and they never should have given up their jobs running the hotel to open up a place of their own. I reckon she's got a point. I mean, no one ever consulted me about whether I wanted my whole life turned upside down just because my parents took it upon themselves to move. They just treat us like we don't have a say in our own lives. I'm sick of being treated like a kid. Anyway, Dad keeps trying to tell her it's only a minor setback, but I had a look at the hole in the ceiling today, and there's nothing minor about that! Finn and Lewis came in to talk to Dad about the lease on the yard. They were all over Beth. I don't know how any bloke in his right mind would fancy her – they should see her first thing in the morning, she's in a right state. There's no way they're getting anywhere near her, though, and I made sure they knew she's only sixteen. Don't know why I bother to look out for her, though, she's being a real pain – she's suddenly realized she's done no revision for her GCSEs and keeps yelling at us every time we make the slightest bit of noise. I can't wait to get out of here after my 'A' levels. I'm going travelling like Adam did – I might not come back at this rate. What's there to come back for? Sometimes I think the sooner I see the back of this place the better.

Monday 24 May 1999 – 11:40pm

I'm dead worried about Beth, she really fancies Lewis big time and he's all over her. I bet he's only doing it cos I took Ruth off him. If he does anything to hurt her I'll kill him. She's got her first exam on Wednesday, geography. I heard Zara testing her last night and she knows naff all. Mum told me that Ruth came into Deva today looking for me. I knew she'd wise up, she knows it makes sense. I went into the college to try and find her and couldn't so I had a coffee with Jas instead. She's alright really, I thought I might go for it for a minute and then I remembered she's been a bit of a bunny-boiler with Adam. Jas didn't know about Ruth wanting to see me but reckons she's really stressed about her exams – I bet she wants me to relieve some of the tension with a bit of the old Morgan magic. I saw Lewis while I was there, thought it might be worth my while to make an effort with him seeing as he's hanging around Beth like a starved dog. He didn't seem that into it at first, but he came into Deva and invited me to a poker game with some of the lads. Don't know why I bothered, he fleeced me – that's probably why he invited me, though, knowing him.

Tuesday 25 May 1999 – 10:27pm

Living in this house is doing my head in. It's just constant grief. This time it's Zara – she's such a pain. She's only gone and got herself suspended from St Mary's for bullying. I've never seen Dad so angry in my life, he looks like he's going to explode. He and Mum had to go and see her headmistress and she reckons it's not the first time, and they might chuck her out. It would serve her right if they did, she's such a spoilt brat.

Sunday 30 May 1999 – 7:48pm

I had to work in Deva today, but it's alright on a Sunday cos no one comes in. It's also nice to get away from the house at the moment cos Beth is all crabby cos of her exams and Zara keeps having yelling matches with Mum and Dad. Adam reckons fat Wayne tried to get him sacked on Friday. His rat drowned in the college swimming pool and he reckons Adam did it to get back at him for the fight. He's so sad.

Monday 31 May 1999 – 9:59pm

I've met her. The perfect woman. A definite 10 out of 10, like someone in a magazine. Her name's Mandy Richardson, she's my age and she does a bit of modelling. A model! Could she get any more perfect? I fancied her like mad from the moment I saw her – though of course I made sure I wasn't too obvious – but I couldn't do that much flirting, cos she was only with Ruth wasn't she? Typical that is, no women for weeks and then two at once. They're like buses. Adam reckons she's well out of my league and bet me £50 I can't pull her. No problem. Get your money out, mate, I've always been up for a challenge, especially one with a bod like that.

Wednesday 2 June 1999 – 10:16pm

Mandy came into Deva again today and she looked fantastic. She is totally gorgeous. I've got to admit I felt a bit nervous when I saw her, anyone would. But I made sure I served her and we had a bit of a chat. At first she seemed really into me, but then she just went cold and flounced out with her nose in the air. Sometimes women are a mystery, even to me. I can tell she's going to need a bit of work. I don't mind though, it's more fun when they play hard to get. I could kill Zara sometimes. She was a total spoilt brat when Mum and Dad told us they can't afford to take us all on a foreign holiday this year. I mean, I was pretty gutted as well but all she was worried about was what her friends are going to think – she's turning into a real snob. Dad wants to send Zara to Hollyoaks Comp next year to save a bit of money but Mum doesn't think it's as good a school as St Mary's. She's so soft on her it's unbelievable. She even thinks that it might not have been Zara's fault she was suspended. Oh really!

Saturday 5 June 1999 – 11:59pm

Jeremy and I went out sharking tonight in town. I wasn't really into it though, none of them were half as good looking as Mandy and most of them are just bimbos who can't take their vodka and Red Bull anyway. I don't know whether it's cos there's the prospect of getting fifty quid off Adam at stake, or just that she's resisted me so far, but I really won't rest until I have Mandy Richardson. Maybe it'll happen next Friday. There's a gig on at the Yard and Mum and Dad are doing a big barbie – that's if they haven't killed each other by then. Why is it they (a) only argue about Zara or Deva and (b) decide to do so when I am trying to go to sleep? I've tried putting a pillow over my head to drown out the noise, but it's no use. They're at it now cos Dad arranged for Zara to go to Hollyoaks Comp next year without telling Mum first. Their arguments always follow the same patterns. I bet there's still about half an hour to go before they shut up on this one. First Mum looks all wounded and hurt, which makes Dad slam around a bit until Mum either tells him to calm down or asks him what's wrong. Then he tells her, then she gets all defensive, especially if it's about Zara. Then Dad starts yelling, then Mum starts screeching, then Dad yells even louder, then Mum starts crying, then Dad comforts her, then she cries a bit more, then he apologises and then they make up. We're at the Mum screeching stage at the moment. I'm not sure I can take much more of this.

Saturday 12 June 1999 – 8:49am

Yesterday was a good day. It's funny how all the grief you've been going through vanishes when something goes right. And that something is Mandy. I finally managed to talk her round late yesterday. It was a bit of a struggle, but after a lot of schmoozing on my part, she told me that Zara had told her all about the bet. I had to do some really quick thinking and told her I made the bet when I first saw her and never expected to like her as much as I do. She looked like she didn't believe me until I told her I'd called the bet off and all I wanted was to get to know her. I'll still cream in the fifty quid off Adam – I'll just have to make sure blabbermouth Zara doesn't know about it. Anyway, she agreed to come to the gig with me which was great while it lasted. It was going really well and I was just gearing up to kiss her when there was a power cut. We hung around for a bit, but I was getting in a really bad mood cos I could see Beth getting off with Lewis. We decided to split and went for a walk along the river. Mandy got a bit cold so I gave her my jacket. We held hands and just walked and walked for ages – it's funny cos I hate walking when I'm not going anywhere usually, but it was nice last night, really nice. I tried to kiss her, but she wasn't that keen. She said she didn't want to rush things. That was cool by me, I mean, just going out with a model is an achievement worthy of major note. Can't wait to tell the lads at school on Monday.

Monday 14 June 1999 – 9:45pm

I'm knackered, I worked really hard at footie practice tonight and stayed on a bit after to do a workout in the gym. I suddenly realized that if I'm planning to get busy with a model in the not-too-distant future then I'd better get myself in shape. Adam's doing my head in a bit, he's such a sore loser. He's refusing to cough up the money he owes me for pulling Mandy as he reckons he has no proof. He's just jealous – jealous, sad and single. He keeps trying to tell me he's got this girl over in Australia who he had a thing with on his year off, but that sort of stuff's easy to say isn't it when there's no way I can ever get proof, and he knows it. He reckons he's going to get her over to Chester for a stay – yeah right, watch this space.

Wednesday 16 June 1999 – 10:52pm

Adam, you tightwad, give me my money! The slimy cheat still won't pay up and it's really starting to get on my wick cos I'm skint and I've got a date with Mandy tomorrow night. Doesn't he realize how important this is for me? Luckily Dad stepped in and gave me my allowance early, though he had a go at us for making a bet on a girl. Parents are so two-faced, I know it was the kind of thing he'd have done when he was our age. What a hypocrite! Mum and Dad are rowing again and for once it's not about Zara. Mum's hacked off with Dad cos he didn't tell her he was going to lease the yard to Lewis and Finn for another six months. She wanted to turn it into some sort of poncey, paved piazza or something. Anyway, they'll jump at any excuse to have a go at each other and fill the house with bad vibes – and we're the ones who end up suffering for it.

Thursday 17 June 1999 – 6:30pm

I can't wait to break up for summer. It's too hot to concentrate on school work and there's so much else to think about anyway, namely Mandy and how to get her into bed. I'm just getting ready for our date but have got a bit of time to kill while Mum irons my shirt for me. For once the house is really quiet cos Zara's over at Steph's, Dad's at Deva, Adam's at work and Beth's revising – well, pretending to anyway. I just went into her room to ask her advice on whether I should get Mandy flowers or not and she was just sitting there on the bed listening to sloppy music with this stupid grin on her face and doodling Beth 4 Lewis on her notebook. Pathetic. Girls are so sad. She said no to the flowers, reckons they're too cheesy, so I gave them to Mum instead, hence her ironing my shirt for me. And what timing, here she is now.

6:35pm

Stupid, stupid woman. I can't believe it but mum's gone and washed the wrong shirt. Now what am I going to wear? She's ruined my evening before it's even started.

Friday 18 June 1999 – 2:04am

The date with Mandy started off as a disaster but ended up a total result. For a start, I forgot it was racing so it was crowded in town and we couldn't get into the restaurant I wanted to take her to – or any restaurant for that matter. I was pretty fed up and she didn't seem too impressed. In the end I got us some chips and we went and sat in a rowing boat. I felt really bad cos I'd had such big plans but Mandy said she preferred doing stuff like that anyway. That's a relief, cos I wondered if she was going to be like all the models you read about who have tantrums all the time, chain smoke and don't eat, but she's not like that at all. She's actually really nice. She explained she was off with me earlier cos she was still a bit upset about the bet and that she didn't want to be a trophy girlfriend. I told her again how much I like her and this time she let me kiss her, and a bit more, but not all the way – yet. It's weird, I've kissed a lot of girls but this time it was different somehow. Usually I'm just wondering if I'm going to get them into bed. But with Mandy I wasn't really thinking about that, even though she's absolutely gorgeous. She looks even better close up and she smells lovely. I must remember to ask her what perfume she wears. Girls like that kind of thing. When we had a snog, she tasted sort of sweet. I actually don't mind if she doesn't want things to move too quickly. I think I like her more for it. Some girls are worth a bit of patience. (God, I've just read this back and I sound like a right soppy twat. Next thing you know I'll be turning into Adam. Help! What's she done to me?)

Wednesday 23 June 1999 – 10:43pm

Beth's in a right strop cos Mum's had a 'chat' with Lewis about their relationship. How embarrassing – she's gutted and thinks he'll never want to see her again, which isn't such a bad thing from my point of view cos I think she could do better than him anyway, but I'd still hate it if Mum stuck her nose in with me and Mandy. Apparently Mum gave her the big sex talk as well, I mean come on, she's sixteen, she knew all that stuff years ago.

Thursday 24 June 1999 – 11:20pm

Something weird's going on with Dad. Adam said he's been to see a specialist today about his blood pressure. I don't know much about that stuff, but I know you don't see a specialist just for blood pressure, there's got to be more to it than that. I hope he's okay. I've got another date with Mandy tomorrow night. She's got us some tickets to go to the college ball. It's a shame Beth's going with Lewis, cos not only will I have my kid sister cramping my style, but I'll also have to contend with Lewis breathing down my neck and watching everything I do. Almost forgot, Mum and Dad had a visit from the police today cos Finn and Lewis found a skeleton when they were digging up the yard. It's been sent away for testing, but they said it's possible it could be a murder!

Friday 25 June 1999 – 7:00pm

Dad is so embarrassing! I've just picked my DJ up from the dry cleaners and dropped Dad's car off for him at Deva, he's so tight not letting me have it tonight. And do you know what he did? He took me into the kitchen and gave me a speech on how to treat girls and to 'be careful'. The birds and the bees? At my age? Talk about teaching granny to suck eggs. As if that wasn't bad enough he gave me a box of condoms to have in my pocket. I mean, does he seriously think I'm going to walk around with a three-pack in my pocket, especially one my dad's provided me with. What if Mandy happened to find them – I'd look like a right prat.

Saturday 26 June 1999 – 10:05am

Last night was a blast. Dad lent me the car in the end on the proviso I took Beth and brought her home again. Luckily she was as into this idea as I was, i.e. not, and I dropped her off at a bar where she was meeting Lewis. I picked Mandy up from her place. I met her mum which was a bit scary cos behind her smile I'm sure she was saying something like, 'You lay a finger on my daughter and you're dead, sonny Jim.' I hate meeting girls' parents. Anyway, there were loads of people at the ball and luckily I didn't see too much of Beth. I wasn't worried about Lewis taking advantage of her or anything cos she was puking her guts up by ten and I saw him taking her home. Ha! That'll teach her. Mandy and I had a great time. We danced loads and then went and found a secluded part of the college garden by the river. We just sat there dangling our feet in the water and snogging for ages, well, until some drunk lads decided to go for a swim and started dive-bombing each other. We came back here at about three and I nicked a bottle of Dad's wine from the cellar and we crept up here. I lit a few candles and put a nice slow CD on and we just lay here half-naked for hours just kissing and stroking. She looked stunning in the candlelight. Cute nose, blue eyes, soft mouth, and her skin's like silk. I was the perfect gentleman – I didn't try it on. I'll know when she wants to, and it made a nice change not to do it straight away. We must have fallen asleep, cos the next thing I knew I could hear Dad mowing the back lawn. I managed to sneak Mandy out without anyone seeing and walked her back home. She said she had a great night and it seemed the right time to ask if, like, she fancied being my girl-friend. I hate all that 'will you go out with me stuff' – it's such cheese on toast – but she said yes anyway. So hopefully I won't have to ask that one again for a long time.

Thursday 1 July 1999 – 11:58pm

Beth's in a right state cos Lewis dumped her – apparently he said it's not her it's him, creep. All she does is cry and play soppy music all day and all night. Mum's making a real fuss of her and giving her loads of treats. I hate Lewis' guts for doing this to her. She's really cut up about it, even though it's not like they were together for ages or anything like that. I heard her on the phone to one of her mates last night going on about how much she loves him and she'd do anything to get him back. I don't know why she's wasting herself on a jerk like him. Next time I see Lewis I'm going to kill him, if Adam doesn't get there first. This is just his style, he gets what he wants then loses interest. I'm pretty sure he was her first as well, what a git. I really think he never liked her in the first place and just did it to get back at me for the Ruth thing. Well he'll pay for it, no one upsets my sister and gets away with it, especially not him.

Sunday 11 July – 8:19pm

Just when I thought Deva can't get any more tacky, Dad does something to top it. The latest is a Roman menu, things like Julius Caesar Salad and Pompeii Potatoes, how naff is that? He reckons the tourists will love it, yeah right. It's all because it turned out the skeleton in the yard was hundreds of years old and now they've taken it to some museum in London for tests. There's all these archaeologists digging the place up and, guess what, they've uncovered a Roman brothel. There's porno mosaics and everything, it's cool. Beth and Zara think it's gross, but me, Dad and Adam think it's wicked. As you can imagine, Mum's not too impressed, she's worried about our image. Stuff that for a game of soldiers, my street cred's in the premiership at school cos of this.

Monday 12 July 1999 – 9:28pm

Lewis is such a moron. He thinks he's so tough, he had a right go at me today about making sure I treat Mandy well. I can't believe the nerve of him after what he did to Beth. I like Mandy loads but it really gets on my nerves the way her family are so protective of her, it's like they think I'm going to turn into a psychopath and murder her or something. I wish Mandy would stand up for me a bit more, I mean, she knows Lewis has a problem with us being together, but she never defends me. I don't know, maybe I'm getting all worked up over nothing, but I hope Lewis doesn't mess things up for us.

Wednesday 14 July 1999 – 10:04pm

Some days I wish I'd never got out of bed. I had a really bad day at school, the teachers are piling on the home-work like it's going out of fashion. We're all winding down and getting ready for the holidays and they're getting all serious on us about next year, you know, treating us like we're in the upper sixth already. I wish teachers would chill out a bit, there's plenty of time to get stressed about

'A' levels next year. Then I went to football and we got stuffed. It's not even as if I can blame anyone else cos I fluffed two goals. I mean, Simon had set the first one up for me perfectly and all I had to do was tap it in. I went to kick it and totally missed the ball. I must have looked like such a muppet. After the match I kept replaying it in my head and I still don't know what happened. To make things worse everyone had a right laugh at me in the changing room. Really embarrassing. Then, to top it all off, I went to Deva to get the car off Dad for my date with Mandy and Lewis comes storming in. I hadn't even done anything and he punched me. I couldn't believe it – there was blood everywhere, then he just left before I even knew what had happened. Dad tried to stop me but I legged it out of there and went after him, I tried to give him a right good kicking but Mandy and her mum pulled me off him. It turns out he reckoned I'd got Mandy up the duff cos he found a used test in their bin. Mandy told him that we haven't even done it yet. I liked the 'yet' on the end of that sentence, it says to me that she intends to – which almost made it worth being thumped in the nose! I didn't have a clue what he was talking about and neither did Mandy. Then her mum looked all sheepish and said it was hers. You should have seen Lewis' face, it was classic.

Thursday 15 July 1999 – 2:34am

I can't sleep cos my nose is killing me. Lewis is going to pay for that one of these days. He only got me cos I wasn't expecting it. Still, Mandy and I went into town tonight and had a great time. I sneaked her back here again and things got pretty heated, we nearly did it but she still reckons she's not ready. What does being 'ready' mean anyway, I mean it's not as if we haven't done other stuff so what's the difference in going the whole way. Neither of us are virgins, and I know she's not a Catholic so it's not like it's a big deal. I think she knows I'm getting a bit frustrated but she said that after what's happened with her mum getting pregnant by Mr Cunningham she doesn't want to take any chances. I told her I had some johnnies, but she still wasn't into it.

11:16pm

Beth is really starting to get boring now. She's still moping about, acting the tortured soul over Lewis. I really don't get what she sees in him, he's a maniac. Even when she saw what he did to my face yesterday she just had a 'my hero' stupid look on her face. Mandy told me Beth gave her a letter to give to Lewis. I wish she wouldn't chase him, it's so embarrassing. It's not just me who's fed up with her either, Zara thinks she's so sad. She's finished her exams now and is meant to be working in Deva, but she's told Mum and Dad that she still feels too delicate – can you believe it! So now I get practically no time to see Mandy cos I'm stuck in there everyday after school, and it's going to be worse next week when I break up cos I'll be stuck in there all the time. I heard Mum talking to Dad earlier, she's worried Beth might be pregnant. That's all I need. If she is, Adam and me have decided we're going to get Lewis.

Sunday 18 July 1999 – 8:40pm

Mandy's really hacked off at the moment about her mum being pregnant. She doesn't want her to keep it. I can see her point, I mean I'd be so embarrassed if my mum got pregnant at her age, it's disgusting. I don't think there's much chance of that though cos I don't even think my parents shag any more, they're too busy yelling at each other. Apparently Mr C asked Mandy's mum to marry him, but luckily she said no. Mandy's well relieved, I mean, can you imagine having that old duffer for a step-dad? I'm surprised he could get it up in the first place, he must be at least fifty. Anyway, I earned myself loads of brownie points. I got Mum to make me a picnic and told Dad I'd go to the cash and carry for him if he'd let me have the car for the day. Luckily he went for it. I picked Mandy up and we drove out to this place called Delamere Forest, where Mum and Dad used to take us when we were kids. It was a beautiful day so we had all the windows open and had the radio blaring. We found a really secluded spot and had our lunch. We just lay there all afternoon doing stuff and sunbathing, it was great. Mandy was wearing this little white bikini and she looked incredible, I mean I know she's my girlfriend and everything, but she has got the most perfect body. Lovely, long, smooth legs, flat little tummy and really nice pert boobs, I couldn't keep my hands off her. We were right by a pond and there was no one around, so I tried to get her to come skinny-dipping. She was nearly up to it until we were invaded by a load of OAP ramblers.

Monday 18 July 1999 – 9:53pm

I don't know why anyone bothers going to school in the last week of term, nothing ever happens. I feel like I haven't seen Mandy for days, she's looking after her mum while she decides whether or not she's going to keep the baby. It's really hot at the moment and I'm dreading the prospect of working in Deva all summer. I wish I had enough money to go on holiday. Jeremy and some other lads are going to Newquay for a couple of weeks' surfing. I'm gagging to go but I mentioned it to Mum and she reckons they can't afford to pay for me. It's not even that much money! Beth and Zara are always getting treated, but I ask for one thing and get treated like a second-class citizen. It's totally unfair.

Wednesday 21 July 1999 – 11:20pm

At last, I finally broke up today, six whole weeks of summer lying ahead of me, I can't believe I'll be spending it making coffee for strangers. I'm the only person I know who's not going abroad this year, but I suppose it's not all bad cos I'm also the only person I know who's going out with a model – not only a model, an überbabe. There's something going on with Mum and Dad and it's not Beth this time. Mum finally confronted her with thinking she was pregnant and it turns out she never even slept with Lewis. Anyway, Mum got a call today from her old boss who wants her back. Dad's really annoyed she's even thinking about it, cos he knows she's never been as committed to Deva as him. Maybe it's for the best though, I mean it's not exactly normal to spend 24/7 with someone is it? I mean they live together and work together, no wonder they row all the time.

Thursday 22 July 1999 – 9:00pm

Adam told me why Mum and Dad are always rowing and it's nothing to do with Deva. He reckons that Mum almost had an affair with her old boss where she used to work, and when he called the other day to ask her to come back it wasn't just to her old job. I can't believe it, she makes me sick. I mean, for seventeen years you think you know someone and then they go and do something like that. It's Dad I feel sorry for, I know I wouldn't hang around if anyone did that to me. Adam reckons that they only bought Deva to save their marriage. Great, not only do I not get a holiday this year but now I come from a broken home, too. I mean what if they get divorced? We'll have to leave this house and spend half our time with Mum and the other half with Dad. Neither of them will be able to afford a decent place either. Well there's no way I'm spending any time with Mum. If she breaks our family up I'll never forgive her, she can just get lost.

Friday 23 July 1999 – 11:32pm

I didn't get much sleep last night, I just felt so angry with Mum. And what does 'almost had an affair' mean anyway? I remember her old boss now, William. He's a right flash git and he's loads younger than her. I mean, I know I had my thing with Ruth, but I'm meant to do all that stuff at my age and, anyway, she's only a few years older than me. But Mum and him, it's gross. I'm so glad it's the summer holidays at the moment and all my friends are away cos I'd be the laughing stock otherwise. Anyway, it got to about one in the morning and I still couldn't sleep so I called Mandy on her mobile. She was a bit tetchy at first cos I'd woken her up, but when I told her what was going on she was lovely. She said her Mum was staying with her auntie for the night and Lewis was out with Finn so I went over. It would have been the perfect opportunity for us to do it, but for once in my life I didn't feel like it. We went to her room and just curled up in bed. It was really nice, a bit cramped in a single bed but it felt so great to hold her all night, really safe. I think I might love her. No, scrap that, course I don't. I had to get up mega early to sneak out before Lewis saw me, it feels quite good to know I got one over on him.

Sunday 25 July 1999 – 7:45pm

I feel like punching something. How could she do that to me? I feel like such a mug. There I was thinking I loved Mandy and then I find out she's cheating on me. I wouldn't have believed it if I hadn't seen it with my own eyes. She told me she was too busy to see me in my lunch break today so I went to sit by the river and read *Loaded* for half an hour, and there she was kissing and hugging that prat, Sol Patrick. They didn't see me and I was too gutted to go over and say something, but it was pretty obvious what was going on. From now on I am single.

There's no way I'm going to be like Dad and just pretend it never happened. We are so over. I managed to persuade Adam to go into town with me tonight for a few drinks. He keeps talking about the Kerri girl he had a thing with in Oz, but I told him he should forget about her, I mean you can't get busy with someone who's a million miles away. Things have been very quiet with him on the totty front recently so we're going to go out on the pull next week. Stuff Mandy.

Monday 26 July 1999 – 11:34pm

It turns out Mandy might not have been cheating on me after all when I saw her with Sol. She reckons she was talking to him about some mate of his who killed himself or something and he was really upset. She was really miffed when I accused her and she got really upset. I didn't really realize how much she likes me till I saw how gutted she looked when I accused her of cheating. We went out tonight, just the two of us and had a really nice chat, even though I couldn't help being off with her after all that stupid Sol stuff. The thing with Mandy is, when I first saw her poster I just thought hubba hubba, but she is so easy to talk to and really funny. There's no way she'd cheat on me, especially with that little squirt, as if.

Tuesday 27 July 1999 – 11:29pm

Finn's taking his bus to Cornwall for the eclipse and he's selling tickets as well. I really wanted to go. I thought it would be great for me and Mandy to spend a few days camping down there but she wasn't into it cos she doesn't want to leave her mum. Oh well, I doubt whether that old tin can will make it anyway. I wish I had a car.

Wednesday 28 July 1999 – 1:25am

Mum and Dad spent all day and all night yelling at each other again. Beth and Zara are staying with Richard and Fiona in France for a few days so they haven't got a clue what's going on. I'm getting so sick of this, it's hardly relaxing hearing your parents rip each other to pieces nearly every night. I'm going over to Mandy's again. I can't sleep here.

8:39pm

Everything seems a bit quieter round here today. Mum and Dad haven't had a single row. Adam reckons it's not a good sign, quiet before the storm and all that. He thinks it might be better if they do split up cos then we won't have to deal with them yelling at each other all the time, but I don't. It'll just mess everything up. I went to Mandy's again last night. She's a bit fed up cos not only has her mum decided to keep the baby, but she's also going to marry Mr C. We had a really long talk about parents. Hers are divorced, but she never seems to talk about her dad or see him even, for that matter. I think she must blame him for the split cos she really hates him, she'll hardly even talk about him. She agrees with Adam that if Mum and Dad aren't getting on then it might be better for everyone if they're apart. She said that when your parents do decide to split up it just feels like a massive relief. I think divorce is lazy though. I mean Mum and Dad have been married for twenty years and had four kids. I know it can't be all hearts and flowers after that long, but why throw it away? I mean, they have a history together and it's their job as parents to make sure we're okay and we're happy. All they're thinking about is themselves. Well, it's not just a marriage they'll be smashing up, it's a whole family.

Friday 30 July 1999 – 9:17pm

Adam's mystery Australian girl turned up in Deva today – she's called Kerri and he didn't even know she was coming. The first thing she did was slap him round the face – sounds like my kind of girl. Mum put her in Beth's room cos she doesn't want them doing it in her house, but I heard them at it this morning. It's not fair, I wish I was allowed to have Mandy to stay. I suppose the one good thing about having a guest in the house is that Mum and Dad aren't rowing, they're on their best behaviour. How come they care more about keeping a stranger happy than their own family?

Sunday 1 August 1999 – 11:38pm

Dad walked in on Adam and Kerri in bed this morning, right at the crucial moment as well! He's really embarrassed 'cos he saw Kerri's boobs, but she doesn't seem to be that bothered. Wouldn't mind having a peek myself. I can't believe they're actually shagging just a few feet away. Wonder what the two of them get up to. Whatever it is, they keep pretty quiet about it, which is weird cos Kerri looks like a bit of a screamer to me. Maybe she's in need of someone like me who knows what they're doing in the sack. I can't imagine Adam's all that in the sex department. Beth and Zara got back from France this morning. Beth's really hacked off about Kerri being in her room, I would be, too, if I had to share with Zara. Mandy came to watch me play football this afternoon then we went into town. She's still all wound up about her mum getting married and she reckons she's not going to go to the wedding. I don't really get her problem with it – I mean Mr C's a bit of an old fart, but she could do a lot worse than him.

Thursday 5 August 1999 – 10:14pm

Mum and Dad are rowing again and, as if that's not bad enough, so are Beth and Zara. They've been sniping ever since they got back from France cos Beth got off with some bloke Zara fancied. I wish they'd just grow up, it's impossible to get any peace in this house. I'd go round to Mandy's for the night, but she'd probably do my head in even more at the moment.

Saturday 7 August 1999 – 4:30am

I feel really weird, we've just got back from Mr C's stag night. It was a good night until Sean told me some stuff about Mandy that I just cannot get my head round. Just when you think you know someone almost as well as you know yourself, than bam, someone drops a bomb- shell and you realize you don't know them at all. I wish it wasn't true, I really do, but apparently she was sexu- ally abused by her dad when she was little and never told anyone, then a few years ago he raped her. I just can't believe it, this is the sort of thing that happens to other people. This is serious and I feel totally freaked out by it. Sean said that she ran away to London to get away from him and ended up working in a strip club. I feel numb, I don't know what to think.

5:10am

Can't sleep. I keep thinking of Mandy and I just want to go and see her and give her a massive hug. I wish she'd told me about it herself, I mean there was almost a look of satisfaction on Sean's face when he told me, like he was thinking, 'I know something about your girlfriend you don't know'. I don't know what to do. I want to help Mandy and support her and to let her know I know, but then if she wanted me to know she would have told me. I do feel hurt, I mean I thought we were getting on really well, I thought we were getting close, but this is a pretty massive secret to keep from someone. Maybe she just didn't know how to tell me.

6:34am

There's not much point even trying to go to sleep now, there's too much stuff going on in my head. I under- stand now why Lewis is so protective of Mandy. Just the thought of Dad doing any of that stuff to Beth or Zara makes me feel sick to my stomach. I mean, getting raped is horrible in itself, but by your own Dad, that's just sick. What kind of pervert does something like that? And where was Lewis then, hey? It's alright for him to be like a bodyguard now, but where was he when she really needed him? I'm never going to moan about my family again, we've got it easy compared to what Mandy's been through. I'm going to talk to her after the wedding.

8:39pm

I don't think I handled talking to Mandy very well. She just threw me out of her flat. I might as well start at the beginning. The wedding reception was fine and Mandy seemed okay with the whole marriage thing in the end. She looked really good in her bridesmaid's outfit. I was working cos Adam's done yet another disappearing act with Kerri. I just kept staring at Mandy's mum and in the end Dad sent me into the kitchen to do the dishes cos people were starting to notice. I didn't mean to be rude, I just don't get how could she not have known what Mandy's dad was doing to her? I just think you'd have to be blind not to notice if your husband was touching your daughter up. It's so, so sick. I mean, what if she was in on it too, maybe they were like Chester's answer to Fred and Rose West. I know it's wrong of me to blame Mandy's mum, but it's not Mandy's fault, she was just a kid. Anyway, when the party had finished in Deva, Mandy invited me over to the flat cos she's there on her own tonight. We had a few drinks and we were snogging and that and things got a bit heated. I could tell Mandy wanted to do it, but I just didn't feel comfortable, not like

I don't fancy Mandy any more or anything like that, just that I wanted to talk to her, to tell her I know. I told her what Sean told me and she just went mad, it was frightening. She was crying and shouting at the same time that I had a lucky escape finding out she was damaged goods before I slept with her cos now I don't have to. I told her it doesn't change how I feel about her and I just want her to talk to me but she yelled at me and shoved me out of the flat. She says she never wants to see me again. I can't believe it, I'm so gutted. Just the thought of her in that flat on her own being all upset, I feel so guilty, it's all my fault.

Sunday 8 August 1999 – 7:26pm

I went round to Mandy's again first thing this morning. I took her some flowers to apologise for the way I handled things. We made up and everything, but she still wants us to take a break, she doesn't want a serious relationship at the moment. She said she just wanted to have a normal relationship without the past having anything to do with it. Things were fine until Sean told me about Mandy's past. I wish he'd kept his nose out cos she didn't want me to know and I was a whole lot happier before I knew. Everyone's in a right strop in this house today. Adam's biting everyone's heads off cos Kerri turned out to be a bit of a 'free spirit'. Well, that's one way of putting it – she only went and spent the night with Finn on his bus the other night. Just imagine what she's like when she's back home in Oz. No wonder Adam kept going on about her when he got back – they must have got up to all sorts. Now I know why he reckoned the trip was such an education. Dad's annoyed cos Mum made plans to see her old work colleagues and he thinks that means the bloke she 'almost' had an affair with. I couldn't care less about those two at the moment – if they want to beat each other up all the time then that's up to them – I'll be out of here by this time next year, travelling round the world for my gap year, if everything goes to plan, though the way things are going I'm going to have to pay for the whole lot myself. Knowing my luck I'll probably have to work for a year to afford the ticket. Beth's really doing my head in. She's having one of her moping around and crying phases cos she's just found out Lewis and Ruth are back together, and Zara's just Zara, kicking off about anything and everything.

Tuesday 10 August 1999 – 10:45pm

Do you know what? I am sick of doing all the shifts in Deva while Adam stays in bed with Kerri all day, it's not fair. I mean, all my mates are having a great summer, it's not even as if I have a gorgeous girlfriend to spend my wages on any more. My family sucks. Zara's around, but she's not much help, she's always got such a face on she scares the customers away, and when they do dare to order anything off her she's so sarky. Beth's too devastated about Lewis and Ruth to leave the house and just sits in the lounge in her pyjamas all day watching the All Saints video – she reckons the words to *Never Ever* really apply to her life at the moment. Personally, I think the word 'sad' is more relevant, but hey, who am I to have an opinion?

Wednesday 11 August 1999 – 11:56pm

I don't know what all the hype about the eclipse was for, you couldn't even see it. Everyone was standing outside looking through bits of paper with holes in – but there was nothing to see. People were standing on tables, chairs and even the roofs of cars. There was all this talk about it being like the middle of the night and tidal waves and hail storms, but it wasn't even twilight. I bet whoever thought of inventing those cardboard, safe glasses made a mint, though. Suckers, so much for it being the end of the world today!

Tuesday 17 August 1999 – 11:29pm

Saw Mandy today. I went for a run in the park and she was sunbathing with Cindy. At first she told me to get lost, but I told her we needed to talk and Cindy eventually left us alone, but only after I promised I wasn't going to upset Mandy. Why do girls do that, hang around in packs? I told Mandy how sorry I am for upsetting her and that I just wanted her to know she could talk to me about it now I know. She was really frosty at first but then she got really upset cos all this has brought it all back. I tried to hug her but she wouldn't let me at first, but then she just sort of collapsed into my arms and cried her head off. I didn't really know what to do, I mean, what can I say to make her feel better after what she's been through? She told me she's really glad I didn't just leg it when I found out and explained she was acting all cold towards me over the past few days cos she assumed I'd be too freaked to stick around once I knew the truth. She thought it was easier if she dumped me before I dumped her. As if I was going to anyway. It felt so, so good to hold her again. We just sat there on the grass for ages, facing each other, but with our legs either side of each other, hugging and me rubbing her back. In the end we had to move cos it started to rain. I took her home and she said she just wanted to have a bath and an early night. That's fine by me, I'm just glad she's okay.

Thursday 18 August 1999 – 3:49pm

Mandy's asleep, she looks so gorgeous just lying there with the sun on her. I've got the day off today and Dad let me have the car to take Mandy out. We've come back to Delamere Forest for another picnic. Mandy made it this time – it was her idea to come here cos she wanted to tell me about her dad somewhere private. I was quite nervous, not because I'd hear anything that would shock me, cos there's not a whole lot worse than being raped by your dad, just that I didn't want her to feel pressured into telling me. She said she doesn't feel like that, she just wanted me to hear it from her. She said her dad started touching her when she was four or five but she didn't even realize it was wrong until she was about eleven. She just thought she was daddy's special girl. Then when her friends started talking about their boyfriends and what they got up to with them, she got all confused. She said she's been thinking about it a lot at the moment cos something else is going on. I didn't know what she was going to say and then she told me that Sean's been coming on to her. I knew there was something about him, he's a real slime. She said he told her no one would believe her when she confronted him about it. She told Cindy and Sean was right, he had got to her first and told her that Mandy had been coming on to him, as if. I really want to have it out with him but Mandy won't let me. Maybe I will but just won't tell her, there's no way he's going to get away with this.

11:29pm

I got back from the picnic and walked straight into another row. Mum found Kerri and Adam doing it in the bathroom this morning. I can't believe how much action he's getting, the jammy git! He's humping for England while I'm languishing in the fourth division. I don't reckon he's up to it. She looks pretty insatiable. I'd show her a good time, though. Anyway, Mum's well freaked and thinks Dad should have a word with Adam about sleeping with Kerri in the house, but Dad says that if she's got a problem with it then she should talk to them cos he's not that bothered. I don't believe that for a minute – of course he's bothered, he just wants Kerri to think he's a cool dad.

Sunday 22 August 1999 – 7:23pm

I'm stuffed. Kerri just cooked us all a massive barbecue to say thank you for letting her stay. She's gone to Scotland for a while cos she's bored with Chester. I reckon she's bored with Adam cos he won't do it with her any more now he knows Mum's listening out for things that go bump in the night. I must admit, it would put me off too. Apparently Kerri got in a right huff on Friday cos Adam had a shift at the pool and she wanted him to throw a sickie, so she turned up at the pool, took her bikini off and jumped in, naked. I wish I'd been there to see it. I had a bit of a fantasy about her while she was staying here actually. Sometimes when I hear her creeping into Adam's room in the middle of the night I wish she'd get the wrong room. Not that I don't want to be with Mandy anymore, but can you imagine a girl just coming into your room in the middle of the night, getting into your bed without any clothes on, doing her stuff and then leaving, all without turning the light on? I can!

Tuesday 24 August 1999 – 11:14pm

Beth's still miserable about Lewis, even Mum's lost patience with her. There is one good thing about him getting back together with her though, it means he's hardly ever at the flat. Mandy's mum and Mr C are still away on honeymoon until the weekend, so we're having a great time having the place to ourselves. I stayed there last night. I didn't even tell Mum and Dad I wasn't coming home, all this rowing is doing my head in so much they can have a taste of their own medicine for a change. Anyway, we had a nice night. We went to the cinema to see *Ten Things I Hate about You*, it was okay, a bit of a girl's film, I would have preferred to see *The Matrix*.

Thursday 26 August 1999 – 11:51pm

Mum and Dad closed Deva early so we could have a family celebration for Beth's GCSE results – not that there was much to celebrate, she passed five and only got one 'A' and that was in RE. I can tell Mum and Dad are really disappointed, especially Dad. He reckons he and Mum wasted money on a private education for Beth but Mum reckons she messed them up cos of all that stuff with Lewis. Don't know why she has to try and find an excuse for her, can't she just be thick?

Friday 27 August 1999 – 1:47am

Mum and Dad are having an argument. I was just woken up by Dad slamming the bedroom door and stomping downstairs. Mum's followed him and they're really going for it in the kitchen. I've got visions of one of them doing the other one in with the bread knife.

2:34am

Beth and Zara came in a while ago, neither of them could sleep cos of Mum and Dad, it's only just gone quiet. Zara kept crying. They both think Mum and Dad are going to get a divorce cos Beth crept out to the hallway and heard Mum tell Dad she can't pretend everything's okay any more when their marriage is over and has been for ages. It's never been this bad before, but I'm sure they'll sort it out, they always do. Adam heard us all talking and he came in too. He thinks it's all his fault cos he told Mum and Dad to get their act together and call it a day. He's right though, we're all sick of this constant bickering and I bet that had something to do with Beth getting rubbish results.

2:40am

I don't believe it, the front door just went and I saw Dad's car going down the drive. He's gone.

2:44am

I just went downstairs to ask Mum where he went. She's just sitting on the floor in the kitchen with a huge whisky, crying. She wouldn't talk to me and told me to go to bed. I wish she'd just be straight with me for a change, I'm not a kid any more and I want to know what's going on.

Saturday 28 August 1999 – 11:56pm

Mandy and I finally did it. It feels weird writing that after thinking about it for so long, but then again it did come as a bit of a shock. I went round to her place after my shift cos I couldn't face going home and she told me there was something bothering her about our relation-ship, I thought she was going to dump me, but she took my hand and led me into her bedroom. I was a bit worried at first that she might freak out after everything with her dad, but we took it slowly and it was fine. No, not fine – amazing. It's like we fit together perfectly. There was no awkwardness or trying to impress. It was just... right. Now that it's happened I can't believe we waited so long. I'm glad we did, though. Ruth was defi-nitely right when she told me sex is better with someone you have feelings for. I can see what all the fuss is about now. None of us got much sleep last night cos Dad didn't come back – he spent the night in a sleeping bag on the kitchen floor in Deva. I can't believe it's come to this. He's acting like nothing's happened, but it didn't sound like nothing at half two this morning. Mum's avoiding him, she's refusing to come into work so we're having to do extra shifts – typical. He hasn't come home again tonight either, it's such a nightmare.

Sunday 29 August 1999 – 8:55pm

Dad's still not home. Mum's just as bad as him, acting like nothing's wrong. She went out last night to meet her old boss. She said it was to discuss going back to her old job, but you don't go out on a Saturday night with the man you had a thing with to talk about work. Sometimes I wish she wasn't my mum at all, she doesn't give a toss about us lot. Adam's trying to be all tough about it. I've heard Beth crying herself to sleep every night since Dad left and Zara's just being unbearable. She reckons she's going to refuse to go to her new school unless Dad comes home. At least with Dad not around and Mum out being a tart I get to see more of Mandy. She came over last night and when Mum still wasn't home by midnight I told her she might as well stay. It felt good having sex with Mandy in my bedroom, almost like I was sticking two fingers up at Mum.

Thursday 2 September 1999 – 11:54pm

I can't believe what a snob Zara's being about her new school. It was her first day today and she came home in a right strop, winding Mum up about how much she hates it and moaning that she feels like she hasn't had a summer cos she's used to longer holidays. She can be so selfish, she's oblivious to what's going on with Mum and Dad. All of us keep getting at them to get together to talk but both thinks the other has to apologise first. At least Dad's decided to move into a hotel instead of sleeping at Deva – people were starting to suss him and it was getting embarrassing.

Sunday 5 September 1999 – 7:43pm

I don't know what made me decide to do physics 'A' level. I'm trying to do my summer project on radioactivity and it sucks. I used to want to be an astrophysicist, but I can't face another I don't know how many years of this. I suppose it's better than working in Deva though. That's the only reason why I'm looking forward to going back to school. Kerri's helping Dad out until he finds someone permanent. Got to go, Mandy's at the front door.

Monday 6 September 1999 – 11:34pm

Mandy and I couldn't stay here cos Mum and Beth were having a row about Dad and the whole split – Beth's on Dad's side. Anyway, Adam and Kerri had gone off to the lakes, camping for their last weekend before Adam starts uni, so I nicked the keys to the college pool from his room. I never meant to, I only wanted to borrow some aftershave, but as soon as I saw them, I knew what I had to do. So we waited till it was dark and really quiet and let ourselves in. We could have so easily got caught by one of the security guards but that was half the fun. We took some candles with us and went skinny-dipping. It was really quiet and romantic. It's really nice to make an effort and do stuff that's a bit different when you're with someone you really care about – though it has to be said, doing it under water isn't as easy as it looks in films! The thing about being with Mandy is, that kind of thing doesn't matter. We're so relaxed with each other we can see the funny side. I go back to school tomorrow, I can't believe I wasted the whole summer working in Deva listening to Mum and Dad yelling at each other. When I finish my 'A' levels next summer, I'm definitely going travelling like Adam did. Maybe I'll ask Mandy to come with me, if we're still together then.

Wednesday 8 September 1999 – 11:23pm

School's doing my head in already and we've only been back two days. All the teachers have gone into overdrive and we had a big lecture on how to cope with the pressure of our exams and not stuff up. They handed out UCAS forms almost as soon as we walked in the door yesterday, that's the trouble with St Joe's, they never even consider that some of us might not want to go to university. I mean, I do, but take Ben, for example – all he wants to do is play rugby for England, and he's got what it takes, too. He's wasting his time applying to uni cos he wouldn't get in anywhere decent, anyway. There's no way I'm staying in Chester to go to HCC like Adam, it's not even a proper university. All my mates would laugh if I told them I was going there.

Friday 9 September 1999 – 11:45pm

Weird stuff going on round here at the moment. Mandy's really worried about Cindy's brother, Max, cos he reckons he's seen Sean mistreating Cindy's baby. Mandy believes him, because she knows what a slimebag Sean is from the lies he told about her. The thing is, when Max told Cindy, she didn't believe him – she blamed Max for the kid's bruises. Mandy reckons it's definitely Sean and keeps telling Max to call Childline. I don't know, I'm not sure if she should be getting so involved, I mean, it's not really any of her business. I know it's hard for her to stay out of it, though, cos it's brought back a lot of memories of when her dad was doing stuff to her. Maybe she's right, maybe if someone had intervened when she was a kid, her dad wouldn't have had the chance to rape her. The other thing is that Ruth's ex-husband, Kurt, has died and he was only twenty. He was a lifeguard down south and some bloke was on a jet-ski that went out of control and killed him straight out. The worst part is, the bloke who did it legged it.

Sunday 12 September 1999 – 7:18pm

Mum and Dad got together today for a chat. They decided that Dad isn't going to move back in cos they can't live together, so it took twenty years to find that out, did it? I don't know what Dad's going to do, he can't stay in a hotel forever. It doesn't seem fair, why is he the one who has to leave? I wish Mum'd go, she's no fun, all she does is moan about how Zara's out of control and she's turning into a heathen now she goes to a Comp. Mandy's coming over in a bit, she wants me to help her fill her UCAS form in. I don't know why she's got her knickers in a twist already, they don't even have to be in till December.

Monday 13 September 1999 – 11:13pm

Today's been really depressing. They had the funeral for that Kurt bloke. I saw Ruth, Lewis and the rest of them all dressed in black and looking miserable. I hate stuff like that, makes me feel really uneasy. Mandy said Lewis didn't know whether to go or not cos he and Kurt hated each other. Why do people get so hypocritical about people once they're dead? I think Dad's gone insane, he's only gone and offered Tony a job as chef in Deva. He is so boring, I can't bear to be stuck with him for two afternoons a week after school. I do feel sorry for him at the moment cos apparently Kurt was his best friend. I'm glad I've never known anyone who's my age who's died, it must be so weird. Adam's in a right strop cos Kerri's gone to London for the weekend. I can tell he wanted to go with her but he's got shifts at the pool that he can't miss. I don't know why he ever signed up for Uni – he's done nothing but mope about with a right face on ever since he started. If I was him I'd stick two fingers up and go off with Kerri. She's asked him to go travelling with her again and he's thinking about it. Er, hello? What exactly is there to think about? Get away from all the hassles of home, college work and miserable British weather or go backpacking with a gorgeous blonde who has a penchant for taking her clothes off? I know which I'd choose.

Tuesday 14 September 1999 – 10:28pm

So much for Dad offering Tony a job – he hasn't turned up yet and he was meant to start on Saturday. I mean, I know his best mate's just died, but this is stupid. I was meant to be taking Mandy to see *Never Been Kissed* – maybe it's not such a bad thing as it was another of Mandy's choices! So anyway, I had to work in Deva tonight, but it wasn't too boring cos Mandy came in to do her homework. She's trying to avoid Cindy cos she found out Mandy got Max to call Childline about Sean bruising Holly and she went mad and had a right go at her. Sounds like Mandy and Max did the right thing though, cos Sean legged it yesterday. If you ask me, he definitely did it. I always thought he was bad news. And if he had nothing to hide he wouldn't have scarpered, would he?

Wednesday 15 September 1999 – 11:42pm

Kerri's back. Adam's really annoyed cos she brought Dad a present back from London to cheer him up but she didn't get him anything. I told him he should work on making her feel jealous by flirting with other girls. It shouldn't be too hard round here at the moment cos the place is swarming with freshers, some of them are really tasty too. Adam got chatting to this really sexy girl called Geri yesterday and she's got a great set of wheels. I wish I had a car. I never get a chance to use Dad's these days cos he's not at home and I wouldn't be seen dead in Mum's. Maybe I should start dropping a few hints for them to buy me one, after all, they've got to be feeling guilty for everything they've put us through haven't they? Tony still hasn't turned up and Adam is majorly hacked off with him cos he has to work tonight and he was meant to be going out with Kerri. I think she's had enough, she told him she's going back to London in a few days cos she thinks Chester's boring. She's flying out to Thailand in two weeks and she wants him to go with her. If it wasn't for Mandy, I'd go. The more I see of Kerri, the more I think she's wasted on Adam. She needs someone with a bit more fire in their belly. I'd offer my services but I wouldn't want to do anything to mess things up with Mandy. I've got to get used to being a one-woman man.

Sunday 19 September 1999 – 8:43pm

Mandy's great. She bought me a really cool pair of shades yesterday cos she got paid for one of her modelling assignments. We went to Blackpool for the day and ended up staying the night cos neither of us wanted to go home. Mandy's got Cindy's mum on her back cos Cindy and Holly have disappeared with Sean and no one knows where they are. I couldn't face going home cos Zara, Beth and Mum are all premenstrual. We went on a few rides at the fair and messed about a bit, then we got some beers and some fish and chips and went and sat on the beach. It got really cold and we'd missed the last train so we ended up staying in a really tacky B&B with pink frilly curtains and psychedelic pictures of poodles and teddy bears. The decor was really kitsch, but at least we got a double bed. It's the first time we've had one and it really makes a difference. Mandy had bought dessert cos I bought the chips and booze. We got into bed, and ate ice cream – actually, we ate it off each other, tastes better that way!

Wednesday 22 September 1999 – 10:16pm

Tony eventually turned up for work the other day but he keeps disappearing again. I can't understand why Dad stands for it – he says he's a really good chef, but he can't be the only one in Chester. Adam was gutted yesterday cos Kerri went to London. He's still got just over a week to decide whether or not to go, but I don't reckon he will. Anyway, I've got a sneaky feeling he's got his eye on someone else already. That Geri girl was in again today and she invited him to a party at her halls. I tried to get him to let me tag along but he wasn't into it.

Sunday 26 September – 8:45pm

I haven't seen Mandy for ages. She and her mum went away to a health farm for the weekend as a special treat. I saw her mum the other day and she looks like she's going to drop that sprog any minute and it's not even due for another few months. Mandy and I had a bit of a fright the other week cos she forgot to take her pill a few times and then her period was late – it was only a few days, but they were the scariest days of my life. We've decided to go back to using johnnies as well, just to be on the safe side. I don't mind really, whatever keeps her happy. It seems like Beth's finally got over her infatuation with Lewis. She's just started seeing someone else, who I presume she met at college. None of us have met him yet, she's keeping things pretty schtum for now, but I do know he's called Rob. I'm glad she's happy – anyone's got to be better than Lewis and at least it stops her moping about the house all the time worrying about Mum and Dad. I wish Zara would sort herself out though, she's being extra surly at the moment, you know, acting a real tough nut and always trying to get the last word. I think she might be smoking, too – she came in the other day and absolutely stank. Mum's so wrapped up in herself she didn't even notice. Well it's up to her, she's the one who's going to have to pick up the pieces when Zara goes off the rails.

Tuesday 28 September 1999 – 12:47pm

I've got loads of school work on at the moment plus football training. All I seem to do is work these days. It feels like we used to be pretty well off, but just because Mum and Dad decided to go completely mental, I end up having to work like a dog while everyone else is enjoying themselves. It really bugs me how Dad expects me to spend every spare minute slogging my guts out in Deva. I know it's good to have a bit of money, but most of my mates get that much as an allowance. I keep worrying that Mandy's going to meet some bloke who's got a flash car and loads of cash to spend on her. I'm saving up for some wheels, but it's going to be years before I can afford anything decent on what Dad pays.

Friday 1 October 1999 – 7:23pm

Can't be long cos I'm just about to go and meet Mandy in town – we're going clubbing with a few of my mates and a few of hers. She reckons Jeremy's really going to go for her friend, Sarah. Knowing Jez he'll go for anything with a pulse. I'm taking my toothbrush with me so I can stay with Mandy cos it's like a war-zone round here. Zara stayed out with one of her mates last night and didn't tell Mum where she was. She was going through the roof till she called Hannah's mum and she told her Zara was there. I know I've stayed out before, but it's different for blokes, we can look after ourselves. Besides she's just a kid.

Monday 4 October 1999 – 11:32pm

How come Beth can never go out with someone normal?

Ruth had a chat with Adam at college today and she told him all about this Rob Hawthorn bloke Beth's been going out with. Apparently he's even older than Lewis and he's been in loads of trouble with the police and got one of her mates hooked on heroin. Ruth said she reckons he killed Kurt. I don't see how he could have done, but Adam says she was deadly serious. She reckons we should make sure Beth has nothing to do with him cos he'll mess her up big time. Adam told Beth what Ruth said and warned her off him but she said Ruth's lying cos she hates Rob. Beth says she's talked to Rob about it loads, and the reason Ruth hates him is cos while she was still married to Kurt she had a bit of a thing with Rob, and she got all guilty and was terrified he'd tell. That kind of makes sense, I mean, I know from personal experience that she's not exactly the faithful type. It all seems a bit far-fetched to me, all these stories of heroin and murder, don't know why Ruth would make something like that up, though. Me and Adam are going to ask Beth if we can meet him so we can suss him out for ourselves.

Wednesday 6 October 1999 – 11:12pm

No one's interested in anything I do in this house. I scored a hat trick today and Mum hardly even heard me when I told her, she was too busy having a go at Zara cos she's been skiving again. She is such a pain, why can't she just get on with school like the rest of the world? She reckons she's not learning anything at the Comp and that the teachers are rubbish. She does all her complaining to Mum to get her on side cos she knows she never wanted to send her there in the first place. She's being such a brat to Dad, she had a right go at him the other day and told him it's all his fault she's like she is cos he's the one who messed everything up. I'm not quite sure how she came to that conclusion, but I can't be bothered to try and find out. Beth's in a bit of a state about Mum and Dad. She's really upset cos Dad's staying in a really ropey B&B and he even has to share a bathroom and kitchen. She kept asking if she could go and visit him there but he wouldn't let her, so she just turned up on his doorstep yesterday. He was pretty annoyed that she'd disobeyed him, but I think he was more embarrassed about where he's staying than anything. Beth says the carpet's threadbare and he's only got a single bed. Apparently there's no phone and there's not even a washing machine. I wish he'd come home. I don't think Mum's got any idea what she's done to him.

Thursday 7 October 1999 – 10:51pm

Seems like Ruth and her mates aren't going to let this Rob Hawthorn thing drop. Beth finally let us meet him today. She brought him into Deva this evening. He seemed alright, he's a bit posh and could do with cutting his hair, but he's not the psychopath Ruth told Adam he was. We were having a drink when Ruth, Tony and that Lucy Benson came bursting in. They were all yelling and screaming at Rob, and Lucy was even trying to hit him, it was mayhem. Dad shouted at them to get out, but they wouldn't go. Rob looked really embarrassed and he offered to leave himself but Dad wouldn't hear of it. He eventually got them all out, but they were still making a fuss, so he barred them all and sacked Tony. I haven't seen him so angry in ages, well, not since the fight with Mum the other month.

Saturday 9 October 1999 – 11:43pm

Had to go into school this morning for a detention for not turning up to general studies three weeks in a row. I don't see why we should have to take it anyway, it's so boring and the exam's going to be the luck of the draw anyway cos it's all multiple choice. I'm so sick of being treated like a kid – it's not as if I even had a choice about whether or not I took three 'A' levels. I'm really bored, Jez is on a geography field trip and Mandy's doing one of her modelling assignments. I wish she was only a hand model or something, I hate the thought of other blokes getting off on seeing her in her bra and knickers in those catalogues. Dad's definitely going soft in his old age. He's only gone and given Tony his job back. Beth's mad about it, you should have heard some of the stuff he was saying about Rob. Dad doesn't seem so sure he likes him now though, cos Lucy came to see him. Can you believe it, apparently she's the one Rob got hooked on heroin! It's weird, you know stuff like that goes on out there, but when it's someone you kind of know, someone who lives just down the road, that's freaky. Dad won't say much, only that he had a good talk with Lucy and he has every reason to believe she is telling the truth. He says he's got his eye on Rob and if he makes one false move he'll be out of Beth's life. I think he's being the over-protective

Dad if you ask me. I mean, Rob's well dressed and well spoken –he hardly looks like a drugs dealer.

Monday 11 October 1999 – 10:19pm

I'm really worried about Beth. All this stuff people are saying about Rob is really upsetting her. Apparently Ruth practically followed her round college till she stopped and listened to what she had to say about him and it was really horrible stuff. Then she went to do her shift in Deva and Tony did exactly the same. I told Mandy what's been going on and she said the same as everyone else, that Beth should stay away from him. She said he's really twisted and he'll make Beth's life hell. I know Beth likes him, but I'm going to tell Dad what Mandy said, it's for her own safety. I wish Adam was here so I could ask his advice but he's gone to see *Romeo and Juliet* with one of his lecturers. I bet it's that Christine, he really fancies her. He's been bugging Dad to buy him a car recently. I'm really annoyed cos Dad said he'd think about it which means I'm going to have to wait forever for him to get me one.

Wednesday 13 October 1999 – 11:16pm

I ended up staying at Mandy's last night cos World War III broke out at home. I told Adam about what Mandy said and he made me tell Dad. Dad went off his rocker and told Beth she's not allowed to see Rob any more. She told him she's in love with him and he just laughed, not the most tactful move in the world. She got really upset and had a right go at me, I felt pretty bad about it, but I honestly only said it cos I'm worried about her. She didn't stick around to listen to Dad and walked off in a huff. Me and Adam went home and she was there blubbing her eyes out to Mum. Mum reckoned it wasn't fair for Dad to tell Beth who she can and can't see, so she rang him and he came round. When Zara found out Dad was coming over she got well excited cos she thought it might mean he and Mum are getting back together or something dumb like that. Anyway, Dad turned up and they started off talking about Beth and Rob but then it turned into another one of their screaming matches, slagging each other off. I didn't hang around to hear all of it, I just grabbed my school stuff and went to Mandy's.

Thursday 14 October 1999 – 11:01pm

I always imagined the day I got my first car would be one of the best of my life – how wrong could I be? Dad called this morning to tell me and Adam to be at Deva this afternoon cos he had a surprise for us. We knew it would be a car cos he said he wouldn't buy us one each, but would consider getting one between us. I left loads of brochures with him of all the ones I like. You know, I thought if he was spending twice the money then it was bound to be something flash like an MG, an MX5 or a Z3 if we were lucky. And what did we get? A Fiat 126 – it's not a car it's an embarrassment. Mum and Dad think it's funny and say they bought it cos there'll be no chance of us boy-racing in it. No chance of any of the other in it either, it's tiny. I mean, what are all my mates going to say when I pull up in that at school? They'll just laugh at me, it's a joke. Mandy teased me loads, which I didn't mind, but Ruth's brother, Darren, has just moved back to Chester from the States and he had a right laugh at me. I don't like him, he's too cocky and you should have seen the way he was flirting with Mandy.

Friday 15 October 1999 – 11:14pm

Just got off the phone to Mandy, she's away again this weekend. She's got a modelling shoot in Prestatyn – we never get any time together at the weekends.

11:27pm

Something weird happened today, Mum asked Dad to move back in. I don't know what is going on there, especially as she's been working so many late nights recently. She always used to say she was working late when she had that thing going with her boss. I just realized, she's working with him again. How stupid was I to hope she asked Dad to move back in cos she wants a reconciliation – she probably just wants someone to baby-sit Zara while she goes off being a tart.

11:40pm

Yup, I'm right. I just went and asked Adam about Dad moving back in and he told me not to get too excited cos he's only moving into the spare room. Mum is so selfish, it's all her fault that this family's in the mess it's in.

Saturday 17 October 1999 – 7:30am

Woke up early cos I had a brainwave in the night. Mandy's staying at a posh hotel for her shoot and it's all expenses paid. I'm meant to be going away with my mates to Ben's parents' place in Abersoch, but I'd much rather be with Mandy so I just phoned her and told her I'd drive her – she thinks it's a brilliant idea. We've got to be careful to make sure no one susses though.

3:42pm

I'm bored. Mandy's been prancing around in her bikini with all the other models for almost four hours and they still don't look close to finishing. I hate the way the photographer flirts with her, and she's just as bad. I know she's always telling me that's her job, but does she have to be so overt about it? Anyway, we got away this morning without anyone guessing what we were up to. When Adam realizes I've nicked the car he's going to go ape – serves him right, he's hogged it up till now. It's so nice to be away from all the hassles at home, I can't wait till Mandy finishes up here and I can have her all to myself.

Sunday 18 October 1999 – 11:25pm

I'm knackered. We only got back a couple of hours ago and then I had to face a tirade from Adam about nicking the car. No one seems to have guessed I was with Mandy all weekend though, so that's one good thing. The hotel was incredible, we were upgraded to a suite cos someone had cancelled. We had a four-poster bed, a stereo, minibar and four phones. The bathroom was the size of the bedroom with a shower big enough for the whole football team, plus a giant bath. We had a great time. We had a meal with the other models and photographers in the restaurant and they were all up for a big night in the bar, but Mandy pretended she had a headache and we went back to our suite. While Mandy was taking her make-up off, I got a bottle of wine out of the minibar and lit some candles that we'd brought with us. I put some music on the stereo and turned all the lights off and then ran us a really deep bubble bath. We drank most of the wine while we were in the bath but then Mandy found the switch to turn the jacuzzi on and things got a little heated. We did it twice in the bath, Mandy had to go on top cos I nearly drowned her when I did. When we got out of the bath we put our bathrobes on and sat in front of the fire and finished the wine. We got a bit hot, so we did it on the bedroom floor, then Mandy got cold so I carried her to bed. It was about two in the morning by this time, but Mandy just couldn't get enough of me. We must have done it about six times and then again this morning, I wish we could have stayed there a bit longer. Things aren't so great now we're back. On our way home Mandy realized we were near the caravan park where Cindy and Sean are staying and she begged me to stop so we could visit. I didn't really want to, I can't be bothered with either of them. I mean, Sean's a prat and Cindy's just stupid for being with him in the first place. We did stop and it was really awkward for a while. Cindy was trying to pretend that everything's brilliant with them when it's so obvious it's not. For a start, Cindy had her arm in plaster. Both me and Mandy think Sean did it.

Mandy's annoyed with me for telling them about our weekend and how brilliant the hotel was, but I couldn't help it, they just depress me so much – I never want to be like them. Sean and I went to the pub for a bit to give the girls a chance to catch up. He wasn't as bad as I'd remembered – in fact he even said sorry for spilling the beans about Mandy and her dad. He reckons it was to warn me not to come on too strong. He also said that Mandy's had a few problems thinking that men are coming on to her when they're not cos she's hypersensitive about blokes. He reckons that's why she thought he was coming on to her but assured me he wouldn't – why would he when he has Cindy. Well, he just answered his own question in my opinion. Our weekend was a bit spoilt by seeing those two. Mandy was really hacked off when I told her what he'd said. I told her I still think he's a moron but it was too late, she got in a right strop. I wish I'd never mentioned it now.

Friday 22 October 1999 – 10:30pm

I'm working in Deva. I can't believe it, it's half term and everything, and still I have to slave my guts out in this dump. Zara's doing my head in. She was skiving school again loads last week and Mum and Dad have punished her by making her work here with me tonight – they don't seem to realize that it's more of a punishment to me than it is to her. She's got all excited about Dad moving back in and reckons it's only a matter of time before they get back together, even as I write this she's on the phone to one of her mates trying to hatch a plan.

Why are girls so stupid? It's not going to happen and no matter how much me or Beth or Adam say it she still reckons she's going to succeed. Yeah right, then why's Mum 'working late' again then?

Sunday 24 October 1999 – 11:39pm

Mandy's really hacked off with me cos I said I'd take her out to Delamere Forest today but Dad made me work in Deva. Not only that, but Adam's nicked the car to get me back for last weekend so we couldn't even go out after we finished. Mandy's organising a college calendar to sell for Young Enterprise and she's asked me to be one of the models. I told her I'd only do it if I could be August cos that's the beginning of the football season. She's going to call it HCCY2K – pretty catchy that.

Thursday 28 October 1999 – 11:55pm

I'm staying at Mandy's for a few days while Lewis is away. It's great to be away from Zara, she's in such a foul mood. She spent all day today in her pyjamas massacring pumpkins cos she's having a horror video night with her mates on Sunday. I asked her why she was being so brutal with the spoon and she said she was imagining it was Mum's head – nice. She's being a real bitch to Mum too. I know she blames her for the separation, we all do, but I wish she'd just get over it.

Halloween Sunday 31 October 1999 – 3:04am

I can't sleep. Mum's definitely seeing William, her old boss, again. I knew she and Dad weren't going to get back together, but I kind of hoped. The reason why Zara's been in such a mood the last few days is because she saw them together. She doesn't know who William is but she described the bloke she saw Mum being all lovey-dovey with and it has to be him. I feel more sorry for Dad than anyone. I mean, I lost respect for Mum when she threw Dad out. He's been putting a brave face on it, but I think he's secretly hoping too. Adam's blocking it out, he's gone to a fancy dress party at the halls with that lecturer he fancies. There has to be something up with Beth, cos she turned down an invitation to a party and volunteered to work in Deva tonight. I reckon there's a bloke behind it – I wouldn't be surprised if she's still seeing that Rob on the sly. The way I'm feeling I don't even care – she can't say she wasn't warned if it all goes tits-up. I can hear Zara crying in her room next door, she does a lot of that at night. I wonder if she knows I can hear her? I'd go and talk to her, but I really can't be bothered any more. I'm just so tired with this whole Mum and Dad thing, and I'd probably get yelled at anyway.

Monday 1 November 1999 – 11:23pm

I knew that Rob Hawthorn was bad news. The police came into Deva yesterday to talk to Beth about him – apparently he attacked Tony's dizzy flatmate, Carol, while she was in the bath last night. Beth said she didn't know where he was cos they broke up weeks ago, I hope she's telling the truth, she looked pretty worried. Mum's on my case about filling in my UCAS form, as if she cares anyway. She reckons I should have applied for Oxbridge – yeah right, there's no way I'd get in. I hate the way she pushes us into stuff we don't want to do. Why can't she just accept none of us are ever going to be brain surgeons? She went mad at me when I told her I wanted to have a year out. She says I should apply for courses and make sure I secure a good first choice and then I can always defer. I'm not even sure I want to go to uni at all the way I feel at the moment. I mean, the thought of writing essays for another three years makes me want to puke.

Saturday 6 November 1999 – 6:21pm

I had a great night with Mandy last night. We drove to Liverpool to watch the fireworks at the Albert Docks and then she treated me to dinner cos she's just been paid for her modelling job in Prestatyn. I really wanted to stay the night at her place cos it's a nightmare at home at the moment, but Lewis had Ruth over so I couldn't, and anyway, Mandy's got her period. She's gone to see her aunt with her mum for the weekend so I'm stuck here doing my homework. Why is chemistry so boring? I mean who wants to know about this stuff anyway? Dad is also on my case now about the importance of getting good grades – he must have had an ear-bashing from Mum. He reckons I should cool things with Mandy for a while so I can concentrate on my school work. Like that's a good idea – not! I can't believe he's so bothered, I mean going to university didn't do him much good did it when all he's amounted to is running a duff cafe. Adam's hacked off as well cos Mum and Dad reckon he's wasting his time doing a media degree. There's nothing like parental support.

Sunday 7 November 1999 – 11:40pm

Mandy came round and saved me from terminal boredom last night. She brought some beer and pizza and then stayed the night. Sometimes Mum and Dad are so dense, they don't even realize what's going on right under their noses. Adam reckons if they paid each other more attention now Dad's moved back, then they might get back together. He was asking Dad all about how they first met and all that stuff earlier. Adam's trying to get Dad to cook Mum a candlelit meal. I think it's a bad idea. Anyway, if she's seeing William again then he's better off without her. I reckon we should tell Dad she's seeing him again so he doesn't make a fool of himself but Beth and Adam made me promise not to. I'm going to have to stay up really late tonight cos I haven't finished my chemistry homework yet.

Wednesday 10 November 1999 –11:53pm

Everyone's in a right strop. I knew it was all going to go pear-shaped. Dad agreed to cook a meal for Mum and it was ruined when she came home late. They had a bit of a barney cos Dad thought he was the only one making an effort. Then Mum had this huge go at him cos she thinks he thinks she asked him to move back in cos she wants to get back together with him, which she doesn't. Tell us something we don't already know. Then Dad got all defensive and had a go at her about why she was late when she knew he was cooking for her. He insinuated that she was with William, so he must suspect she's seeing him again even if he doesn't know for sure. It turns out she had to go to Zara's school to talk to her teacher cos she's been skiving again. Dad went mental with Zara and made her cry. She had a go at Dad saying he was kidding himself if he thought he was going to get back together with Mum cos we all know who she'd rather be with. Dad wanted to know what she meant but she chickened out and went off to sulk. Dad told Mum he thinks she spoils Zara and then Mum got all defensive and told Dad she reckons Zara's unhappy at the Comp, and they should find her another private school. It ended with Dad going down the pub and Mum smashing plates in the kitchen. Another normal evening in the Morgan household then! And they wonder why I can't concentrate on my schoolwork – it's going to be their fault when I fail my exams.

Thursday 11 November 1999 – 11:11pm

Everyone's hacked off with Zara about last night. Adam had a go at her for being so selfish and nearly telling Dad about Mum and William. I must say I kind of agree with her, though, he does have a right to know. Beth's really fed up with her cos she's ruined her plans of getting Mum and Dad back together, I don't think any amount of interfering on her part's going to do that, though. I wish she'd just get over it. I was glad to get away from them all this evening, it was my turn to work in Deva after school. Mandy came in to see me and was really frisky – she wanted us to do it in the stock-room, but I couldn't relax. I mean, don't get me wrong, I like living dangerously and all that, but I think it would finish Dad off if he walked in and caught us at it amongst the bread delivery! Tony wasn't in this evening, he said he had some kind of emergency at home. The next thing we knew he was dragging his mattress into the yard and setting fire to it. I thought he'd really lost it, but Mandy told me Lewis told her that Finn and Carol had been using his bed while he was out and now they've both got the scratchies down-stairs. I wouldn't be surprised if they caught something from Tony, not the other way round. Eurgh, makes me itchy just thinking about it!

Wednesday 17 November 1999 – 10:55pm

I stayed at Mandy's last night and we were in bed this morning when Lewis came home. Not only that, but he came in to Mandy's room and I had to hide in the wardrobe, I only managed to get out to go to school cos Mandy asked him to fix the shower for her. She's dead chuffed at the moment cos college liked her idea for the calendar and cos Cindy's finally seen sense and left Sean. Apparently they had a huge bust up on bonfire night and he burnt Holly's hand. He's a right creep – she's better off away from him. Mandy's a bit hacked off with me cos I told her I can't see her tomorrow night. I told her I had extra football practice, but I'm really going into town to get her birthday present. Don't know what I'm going to get her, though. I haven't got a clue what girls want.

Friday 19 November 1999 – 11:16pm

Beth and Zara are all excited cos they reckon Mum and Dad are getting back together. Zara seems to think she caught them snogging on the landing last night. Come to think of it, I did hear something in the night but – eurgh, I don't even want to go there. Beth's over the moon, she's walking around with a permanent grin on her face and has told Dad to take Mum out for dinner tonight. At least it means I can go and stay at Mandy's so I can give her her birthday present when she wakes up – oh, and the gift I bought her, ha ha. I hate shopping for girls – when you buy them perfume it's wrong, chocolates and they moan they'll get fat, and according to Beth flowers are cheesy. In the end I got her one of my team's football shirts with my number on it so she can sleep in it. I got a woman at a dry cleaners to stitch 'my hero' on the back of it. That one's kind of a joke present. The real one is a fake Tiffany heart necklace – there's no way I can afford the real thing on what Dad pays.

Sunday 21 November 1999 – 10:56pm

Get this, Mum only asked me if I'm gay today! Can you believe it? She reckons she's worried about the amount of time I'm spending at Jez's and if I want to I can talk to her about it? Get real, as if, they don't call me Morgan the Organ for nothing at school. If it wasn't so cringe-worthy it would have been funny. She said she'll love me whatever I am. I knew if I told her I've actually been staying with Mandy, she'd have done her nut. Why are parents always so far off the mark? Had a great night with Mandy, she loved both her presents and showed me exactly how grateful she was, if you know what I mean! A big group of us went into town and got really bladdered. It was happy hour in the first place we went to so we splashed out on cocktails. I couldn't stay at Mandy's cos she had some of her mates staying over so me and Jez came back here. I told him what Mum thought about us and he thought it was hilarious and was deliberately camping it up at breakfast this morning. You should have seen Mum's face, she didn't know where to look. I set her straight once he'd gone home though, can't have my own mother thinking that of me, can I? That's probably the only thing I love about my mum at the moment, she's so easy to wind up!

Monday 22 November 1999 – 11:14pm

I'm going to kill Adam one of these days, he seems to think he has a divine right to the car just cos he's older than me. I think he's still sore that I nicked it the other week to take Mandy to Wales. I tried to nick it again tonight, but the tight git had nicked the spark plugs. Had a match after school today against Parkway High – we annihilated them, but it was tough cos the ref was a right old duffer. There's this one lad, Mark Gibbs, who plays opposite me and he's always trying to wind me up. All through the game he was trying to pick a fight and deliberately tripping me up. He had a go at Mandy turning up to watch the game and told me she was a bimbo – and the ref wonders why I reacted? Mark reckons Mandy and I think we're the Posh and Becks of Chester – I think it was meant to be an insult, but I wouldn't mind playing for Man U and being minted. Anyway, we went to the pub after and as soon as my back was turned there he was trying to chat Mandy up. I went over and got rid of him for her and then she had a go at me for being rude to him. She reckons he was only being friendly – yeah, right. Anyway, she got in a right strop and went home. I couldn't be bothered to follow her and try to sort things out, not if she's going to side with him. She can get stuffed.

Wednesday 24 November – 7:34pm

I've decided to apply for a place at uni for next year just to keep Mum and Dad happy. Mum had a bit of a go at Adam yesterday cos she agrees with dad that he'll never get a decent job doing his degree. They've sent off for loads of prospectuses for me to look at and it's doing my head in – too much choice.

10:20pm

Okay, I've found the perfect course, environmental science. It looks great, at some unis you can take a year out and go to Australia and study the Great Barrier Reef. You know what that means, loads of rays and loads of surfing – that, I can live with. Now I've decided on a course I suppose I should pick my six choices of unis. Adam was in a really good mood earlier cos he and some of his mates had been playing some kind of truth or dare game and they dared Geri to drive into town naked. I wish I'd been there to see it. He's really annoyed with Mum, though, cos when he got home he heard her being all giggly and intimate on the phone to William. So much for Dad and her getting back together then.

Saturday 27 November 1999 – 8:00pm

I'm knackered, we had extra football training this after-noon cos the trials for the Chester Reserves are less than a month away now. Jez called to see if I want to go out tonight but I can't be bothered. I couldn't stay on the phone too long cos he would have heard yet another screaming match. Why does Dad have to yell so much? He's having a major go at Zara cos she's been skiving again. Still haven't decided which unis to apply to and still haven't spoken to Mandy. I feel like giving her a ring cos I miss her, but she could have rung me but she hasn't, and that can only mean she doesn't miss me. She's probably already seeing Mark, knowing her. There's nothing on telly, I'm going to bed.

Tuesday 30 November 1999 – 11:12pm

There's something going on with Beth and Zara, they're being so secretive, loads of whispering in corners and all that kind of girlie rubbish. Mandy called on Sunday – we sorted everything out, but she thinks I get too jealous. The annoying thing is, I know I do, but I just can't stop myself. I think it's cos I'm usually the one who does the dumping and I'd hate it if she dumped me, especially for a jerk like Mark.

Wednesday 1 December 1999 – 10:56pm

Guess who's got a trial with the Chester Reserves on 16 December! I was the only one picked from Hollyoaks Junior League and I've got a trial in two weeks. Mark was playing dirty through the whole game – you know, tripping me up and doing sneaky, sliding tackles then holding his hands up and looking all innocent so the ref wouldn't book him. He fouled me three times. The first two weren't anything serious, but the third I definitely should have got a free kick. Anyway, he got what was coming to him, I tackled him and got the ball off him and scored a brilliant goal in the last minute of play. That's what clinched it with the scout, I mean, no one could deny it was like a piece of choreography. I got a yellow card for flooring Mark but it was well worth it. He was really acting up, pretending I'd really bust his leg so that the game would go into extra time. In the end it didn't and I was man of the match. Mandy and Adam came to watch and I could tell they were really proud of me,

29 March 1999: I asked Ruth if she wanted to go out some time, but she said her life was 'complicated', whatever that means.

14 July 1999: Lewis went ballistic when he thought I'd got Mandy pregnant. He can be a right yob when he wants.

17 June 1999: Mandy Richardson – a model all to myself!

The Morgan family (left to right):
Beth, Dad, Adam, me, Mum, Zara.

22 November 1999: There's this one Parkway
lad, Mark Gibbs, who plays opposite me –
he's always trying to wind me up.

9 March 2000: Mark keeps hanging round Deva, hassling me and Mandy. I wish she'd just tell him to get lost but I think she likes the attention.

30 December 1999: A visit from Mark's mates.

30 December 1999: Mark's gimps are too chicken to come after me one at a time, they don't even give me a chance to fight back.

17 March 2000: I wish I could sleep, then at least I could forget for a few hours.

especially when the scout invited me for a trial. Mark was still acting up when we left – they called an ambulance for him, can you believe that?

Friday 3 December 1999 – 11:11pm

14 days until the try-outs. At least now I know why Beth and Zara have been so secretive recently – it's cos of Mum and Dad. They're getting back together and my stupid sisters are practically peeing their knickers with excitement. I hate to do the same on their bonfire, but how long's it going to last? Especially if she is still seeing William. Personally I think she's a cow for stringing Dad along, it made me want to puke when I came down to breakfast this morning and saw them snogging over their cornflakes – eurgh.

Monday 6 December 1999 – 11:32pm

10 days to go. Airlift me out of here. Mum and Dad went mental at me this evening. Gibb's mum phoned and told them he's had to have an operation on his tendon. Apparently he'll never play football again – well that's no great loss. The thing is, though, his mum reckons they might sue me. Mum and Dad are really freaked out about it and reckon I should have told them what had happened at the match. How was I supposed to know this was going to happen? I mean, players get injured all the time in football, it's not as if I did it deliberately. Beth and Zara are really hacked off with me cos Mum and Dad

were on their way out for the evening when the call came and now they haven't gone. Zara's annoyed cos now they're rowing again after they were getting on so well, and Beth's annoyed cos she was going to sneak out to meet one of her friends.

Tuesday 7 December 1999 – 10:54pm

9 days to go. Met Mandy before school this morning – she's really worried about the whole Mark situation. I hate it when people are more worried about my problems than I am, makes me feel nervous. She's really fed up with Cindy cos she's only gone back to live with Sean in that caravan. I wonder how long it'll last this time. She's so stressed at the moment, I think I'm going to have to do something about that cos, come to think about it, we haven't done it for almost a week. Mum and Dad have calmed down a bit on the Mark situation – there's still no news even though I had to give a statement to the police yesterday. They're too busy yelling at Beth at the moment cos they just got a massive bill for her mobile. I don't understand why they got her one in the first place. It's asking for it really.

Wednesday 8 December 1999 – 11:59pm

8 days to go. It's all gone pear-shaped with Mandy. We split up today cos she's been talking about me behind my back to Mum and Dad. She told them that me and Mark famously hate each other and that we've had loads

of fights and she 'wasn't sure' if I did it on purpose. Well, thanks a lot Mandy. I was really angry and she got all girly and upset. Then she said that I get too aggressive about football and it scares her. She reckons I get all het up trying to prove myself to her that I'm good at something cos I'm jealous of her being a model. Yeah, as if, why would I be jealous, you hardly need skill and tactics to stand around in your underwear all day looking pretty. I said that to her and she was really offended. That's one of the most annoying things about girls, they think they can say whatever they like to you, but as soon as you retaliate then you're a bastard. Well, if she's going to go behind my back and not support me when I need her, then I don't need her at all. I'm just going to concentrate on football for now, make sure I'm in peak condition for next week.

Thursday 9 December 1999 – 9:42pm

One week to go. Everything sucks. I didn't score any goals in football practice today and I got subbed at half time. Feeling really rubbish about everything. Annoyed cos I can't get Mandy out of my head and I don't want to think about her when I've got the most important opportunity of my life coming up. It's hell in this house at the moment cos I was right about Beth, she is still seeing Rob Hawthorn. Mum found out this afternoon when she answered Beth's mobile, she recognised his voice. They've told her they're not paying her phone bill and she has to work in Deva for free whenever they need her over the Christmas holidays to pay it off. They keep going on at me about Mark as well. I can't even be bothered to argue with them cos they obviously prefer to believe Mandy over me.

Friday 10 December 1999 – 11:30pm

6 days to go. Just when I thought things couldn't get any weirder in this house, another bombshell gets dropped. I can't believe my parents, they're such a pair of hypocrites. Dad was having a massive go at Beth earlier for lying about seeing Rob again and she just lost it and yelled at him about having an affair with Kerri. I laughed cos I thought she was joking, but Dad just went white and said, 'Who told you about that?' Apparently that's the reason why she left. Dad reckons it was only a kiss, but come off it. If a nubile young thing shows interest in a man of his age, he's hardly going to say no, is he? Mum and Dad disgust me the way they carry on. They go on and on at us the whole time, do this, do that, constantly trying to run our lives while they're swanning about doing it with people young enough to be their kids. It makes me sick to the stomach. And they wonder why this family's so dysfunctional?

Saturday 11 December 1999 – 11:12pm

5 days to go. Beth threw a sickie today. I think she's feeling sorry for herself for causing yet more hassle with Mum and Dad, who didn't stop yelling about Kerri till two this morning. I bet she thinks if she pretends she's ill and looks all doe-eyed at us then we won't have a go at

her about it – yeah Beth, dream on. Zara's already planning her revenge. But she doesn't need to bother now cos the most classic thing happened today. Dad came home at lunch time and found Beth in bed with Rob! Can you believe it? She is going to be so grounded for a year for that, Dad can't even look her in the eye. I must admit, I don't feel too happy about her sleeping with a moron like him, but I don't suppose I have to worry, it's not likely to happen again.

Sunday 12 December 1999 – 7:56pm

4 days to go. You know what I said yesterday about Beth being grounded for a year? Well change that to for ever. She snuck out in the middle of the night, presumably to Rob's, and didn't come home till this evening. Mum and Dad went through the roof and they've taken her phone off her and told her she's never to see him again. Do they really think that'll work? I mean, they didn't do much to stop her last night did they? And anyway, what right have they got to impose their so-called morals on us? Jez wanted me to go out with him and the lads tonight, but I'm not drinking till after the trial. It's lucky I'm not with Mandy any more cos I would have had to have abstained from sex, too.

Monday 13 December 1999 – 11:43pm

3 days to go. Mandy came into Deva today, she said we needed to talk. I hate it when girls say that. She said

she'd missed me and it was stupid why we broke up. I agreed with her and said I was sorry, although I can't remember what it was I'm supposed to have done, but sometimes it's just easier to take the blame than get into another row about it. Anyway, the long and short of it is that we're back together which is good, although my abstaining from sex has gone out of the window!

Tuesday 14 December 1999 – 11:17pm

2 days to go. Here's some advice, never listen to a woman when she thinks she knows about football. Mandy persuaded me to go and see Mark in hospital today. She reckoned that if he does decide to sue and it goes to court then it will be in my favour if I had at least apologised. I wasn't totally convinced, but didn't see what harm it would do. So we turned up and he just told me to get lost, he said I'd ruined his career and he was a dead cert to be picked for a trial with the Chester Reserves – yeah right. He was getting more and more wound up, and in the end me and Mandy just left. We'd just got back to the car when his mates appeared from nowhere and started laying into me. They pushed me to the floor and started kicking me in the back. Mandy started screaming, and it was only when some other people started coming over that they stopped. If they think they've ruined my chances for the Reserves then they're wrong. So much for apologising to Mark, I just wish I'd done the job properly in the first place. Things are pretty fraught here, too. If I had my way I would have stayed at Mandy's but she didn't want me to cos she's

got an assignment to do. Beth's still in a major strop about Rob and keeps trying to sneak out of the house, and Mum and Dad have told me and Adam we've got to keep an eye on her and not let her see him under any circumstances. Great, that sounds like I'm going to have a cracking Christmas holiday, just cos they're ineffectual parents doesn't mean we have to discipline Beth. Mum's just gone into her room to talk to her woman-to-woman, I doubt that'll do much good.

11:25pm

Yep, I was right, there was a bit of screaming then the door slammed after Mum. Typical.

Wednesday 15 December 1999 – 11:20pm

1 day to go. I'm trying to get an early night cos it's my big day tomorrow, but I can't sleep. Half of me feels really excited and the other half feels sick with nerves. I'll be so humiliated if I mess this up. I didn't get that much time for practice today cos Mandy phoned first thing this morning in a right state. She said she heard something or someone in her flat in the middle of the night. She was scared that Mark's mates had come to get her or something. I had a look around and there was no sign of a forced entry but I did find the cause of the noises – her flat's infested with rats. She did the typical girl thing and got totally hysterical about it. She's decided to move in with her mum and Mr C. I tried to persuade her not to, it's been so cool us having that flat to ourselves, especially now Lewis has moved in with

Ruth, but her mind's made up. My back's been really sore today thanks to Mark's two morons of brothers. Mandy reckons I should postpone my trial till it feels a bit better. She didn't really get it when I explained that the Chester Reserves wouldn't take too kindly to that. This is really hacking me off now – every time I try to get comfortable my back hurts even more. It shouldn't affect my game tomorrow, but I could do without it.

Thursday 16 December 1999 – 11:10pm

D-day! What a waste of time. All that preparation for nothing. I totally bailed the trials. Mark's brothers turned up to watch and they kept putting me off, you know, shouting stuff about Mandy and all that. It was a disaster, I mean I am supposed to be St Joe's' star striker and I couldn't even get a touch of the ball. Every time I went in for a tackle I just froze and all I could see was Mark in hospital. I don't know, I must be going so soft in my old age, letting something like that happen on a day like today. The selectors kept looking at me like they couldn't understand why I was there. S'pose they were right. I was crap. Needless to say, I didn't get in. I feel completely numb. That was my big chance and I blew it. I'm just relieved I got my UCAS form in on time. We break up tomorrow, I can't wait.

Sunday 19 December 1999 – 8:43pm

Mum and Dad were both out trawling the streets of Chester last night looking for Beth – she'd done one of her disappearing acts again. So I called Mandy to ask her to come round. It turned out she was glad to get away cos Max had all his stinky mates round to watch videos. I stole some of Dad's wine from the cellar and we came up here. It was great to spend the whole night together again – I didn't realize how much I'd missed her.

Monday 20 December 1999 – 11:31pm

Uh oh. Beth's in so much trouble – she and Rob burst into Deva this morning and announced they've got engaged. Can you believe it? She is such a child sometimes, as if she really reckons she's going to marry that jerk one day. I don't think so. Me and Adam had a ten pound bet on how long it'll last. I said a month, he said two weeks.

Tuesday 21 December 1999 – 11:41pm

Today Mandy and I drove up to Delamere Forest and went for a walk. It was really cold and crisp, so we had to stop every five minutes to snog. Mandy didn't want to do anything else cos she didn't want to get frostbite on her bits. Mandy tried to cheer me up about missing out on the Reserves. She said she was really impressed with my Mr August pose in her calendar and she thinks I could do it pro like her. Nice of her to say so and all that, but I'd never live it down with my mates if they thought I was poncing around in a jockstrap for my pocket money.

Thursday 23 December 1999 – 11:43pm

I knew it was a bad idea when Mum let Beth invite Rob over for lunch without telling Dad. You should have seen his face when he walked in and saw Rob in his chair, I thought he was going to have a heart attack. He physically threw Rob out of the house and had a right go at Mum for not supporting him. Beth got in a strop and stormed out after Rob and hasn't been seen since – another typical day then. Had a good time at the ball last night, Mandy looked gorgeous. It would have been great to have stayed with her if she still had the flat, but I didn't fancy trying to sneak into Mr Cunningham's – never know where Max has got a hidden camera in that place. Adam got one of his Christmas presents early – Kerri arrived about an hour ago. I could hear them hard at it so had to get my music blaring, then Dad comes up and had a go at me about noise! I'll tell you one thing, Adam wouldn't go near her if he knew Dad had had his way with her. Eurgh, I can't even think about it it's so gross, but Adam has a right to know. Anyway, they're so busy worrying about Beth they've forgotten about all this Mark stuff, so that's good.

Christmas Eve 24 December 1999 – 9:15pm

At four o'clock this afternoon I suddenly realized I hadn't bought any Christmas presents so I had to nick the car off Adam and go into town. I got Mum, Beth and Zara smellies – unoriginal I know, but it keeps them quiet. I got Dad the *Royle Family* video – I don't know whether he's ever seen it, but I fancied watching it. I got Adam the *Ali G* video, but again, only cos I wouldn't mind having a look at it myself. Boyakasha! I'm going out in a minute with Mandy and a few other people. We're going to try and get into the opening night of this new club, called Juice, in town. Don't fancy our chances much cos we haven't got tickets, but Mandy's quite good at using her feminine charm!

Christmas Day 25 December 1999 – 11:40pm

I hate Christmas Day, it's not natural for families to be squashed up together pretending they like each other for the whole day. I got up early like I always do, to check out how many presents I got. Usually Adam and Beth are there, too, but this year it was just me and Zara. She always gets more presents than the rest of us, it's not fair. Anyway, Beth's been in a right mood all day and we had to wait for ages for her to get ready before we could open our presents – why do girls take so long to get ready? We had to rush through the presents cos Dad had to keep checking on the turkey, which was burning a bit cos we were running so late, thanks to Beth. I got what I wanted from Mum and Dad, a computer with access to the inter- net. I told them it would help me with my homework, having access to all that information – suckers. Adam got me the *Cypress Hill* CD, Beth and Zara got me a book about David Beckham but (a) I hate joint presents and (b) all the pages were bent. Kerri got everyone something from the Australia Shop in Covent Garden. I got a boomerang which is pretty cool, but not as cool as

Adam's didgeridoo. I went over to Mandy's for a while, but the atmosphere there was even more terrible than here due to the fact that Mr Cunningham's first wife still hasn't moved out and Mandy's mum's about to drop her sprog any day now. Anyway, she got back at Max big time for taping her in the shower – she did the same to him, but then put the tape on in front of everyone and pretended she didn't know what was on it. She said the look on Max's face when he realized his whole family was watching him smacking the pony was brilliant. I wish I'd been there, but then again, I kind of feel sorry for him, I mean, it's not as if we don't all do it – just most of us aren't stupid enough to get caught!

Boxing Day 26 December 1999 – 11:13pm

All hell broke loose today when Zara got into a row with Dad and ended up yelling at him about his fling with Kerri – and Adam was in the room. It was awful, he thought it was some big joke until he realized none of us were laughing. He went mental with Dad, he just could-n't believe it especially with all the support he's given Dad over the split with Mum. He told Dad he's a sad old man with a mid-life crisis, who was trying to relive his youth through his son's girlfriend, and now everyone's laughing at him. He then screamed at Kerri calling her a slut and all that. She tried to get round him, but there's no way you can carry on with a girl knowing she's sucked gums with your Dad – it's just not right. So he dumped her and she's heading back to Australia in a few days. She's not staying here though, I think even Kerri knows the meaning of 'outstaying your welcome' at a time like this. Good riddance, I say. She may be fit but she's well dodgy. The other thing that happened was that Beth dumped Rob. I have no idea why, but I find it pretty hard to believe she suddenly took heart and realized we were all right about him all along. I mean, something's not right here, teenagers just don't listen to their parents' advice – ever. It's like one of the unwritten rules or something. Anyway, Adam won the bet so I owe him a tenner now.

Monday 27 December 1999 – 4:30pm

I got out of working in Deva today by pretending to Mum and Dad I've started revising for my mocks. I've been playing on my computer, it's wicked. I arranged to meet Jez in a chat room at four, but so far he hasn't logged on. He's probably busy with Polly, his new girlfriend. She's one of Mandy's mates from college and his mission over the holidays was to sleep with her. Bet he hasn't got there yet! I think I'm going to transfer my diary onto my computer, it's probably safer that way cos I can put a password on it. I'll hide this book somewhere, in fact, there's a loose floorboard under my bed. I might go over and see Mandy.

Tuesday 28 December 1999 – 10:40pm

I've just got an e-mail address. Jez keeps sending me porn attached to my e-mails, he reckons that's what he and Polly were up to last night. Yeah Jez, dream on. Zara's being a royal pain in the bum today. She's gone and got herself a Hotmail address and now every time I log on I get a message saying she's got a million e-mails from her dumb friends. I can't wait till New Year's Eve. Jez's folks have gone away skiing so he's having a party and me and Mandy are staying in his parents' room. It's been ages since we spent the night together. Most other people are going to the party in the yard, that's where all my family'll be. I wouldn't be seen dead spending the Millennium with my family.

Wednesday 29 December 1999 – 11:40pm

My Millennium's going to be even better now cos I got a letter today saying Mark's dropping his case against me. I knew he didn't have a leg to stand on – quite literally since I bust it! I tried to get hold of Mandy earlier. I thought we could go out and celebrate but there's no one at her place and no one at the shop. I thought she might be visiting relatives until she phoned to say her Mum had had the baby. Apparently Mandy had to drive her in Mr Cunningham's driving school car. Poor kid, being born with Mandy at the wheel – she hasn't even passed her test!

Thursday 30 December 1999 – 11:54pm

I got another little visit from Mark's mates today. They're such a pair of morons. Too chicken to come after me one at a time, they don't even give me a chance to fight back. I'll be ready next time. No one gets away with pushing me around.

Saturday 1 January 2000 – 9:35pm

Feels dead weird to write that! Guess what? Rob Hawthorn's dead! Nobody really knows what happened, there's even talk that there was a bomb at the yard cos Finn's bus just exploded at midnight with Rob on it – not quite sure what he was doing there, though. Beth's in a right state, she hasn't stopped crying since she found out and the police have been here to talk to her about Rob and everything. It was scary for a while when we all got home cos no one knew where Mum was. Zara got hysterical cos she thought she was dead, too. Sometimes I wish she was the way she carries on. Guess who she spent the Millennium with? Yep, William. Adam saw them together snogging. Poor Dad. Anyway, I'm determined not to let those two get to me this year. Had a good time at Jez's party, we all got really drunk and Jez puked all over Polly, it was classic. What happened was we all went outside for fireworks at midnight. We were standing on the garden furniture screaming our heads off and Mandy got really excited at midnight and jumped in the air and sent the table flying. We all fell off, no one was hurt, but Polly dropped her vodka slush right down Jez's trousers. Lucky strawberry is Polly's favourite flavour cos she started licking it off. Things got a bit steamy so me and Mandy and everyone else went inside. Next thing we knew, Polly comes running in bawling her head off. She locked herself in the bathroom and wouldn't even let Mandy in. Turns out Jez got motion sickness and puked all over her head at the crucial moment. What a dude!

Monday 3 January 2000 – 11:19pm

Beth's still being a misery, but I'm trying to cut her some slack cos I'm not sure how well I'd cope if one of my ex-girlfriends got barbecued. It wasn't a bomb after all, it was arson, but they don't know who did it. Ruth and Lewis came over earlier to try and get Beth to tell the police what a psycho Rob was and he was trying to blow them all up cos he hated them. Apparently, they might charge Lucy with his murder unless they can prove what Rob was like. Me and Adam told them to get lost, there's no way Beth's getting involved in something like that, she's upset enough as it is. Zara's pretty devastated too, I didn't even know she knew Rob, but she reckons he was really kind to her and they used to go for walks when she was skiving school. Sounds like he was a bit a fruitcake to me, I mean, what does a grown man like that want with a thirteen-year-old girl? I don't even want to type the thoughts that just went through my head. He better not have laid a finger on her.

Thursday 6 January 2000 – 11:32pm

I've been back at school for two days and already I'm sick of it. Everyone's suddenly gone all serious cos the mocks are coming up. Even Jez is in a foul mood since Polly dumped him. When school finished, Mark's mates were waiting for me again, I wish they'd go and annoy someone else, it's getting boring now. Even when they think they've done their worst I just walk away with a bloody nose, I mean it's hardly up there with hospitalization is it? Might have to get Jez to help me out if they come back, they just need one big hiding and then they'd get lost. It's not that I can't look after myself, just that I can't take them both on at once. Looks like Adam's getting over Kerri, he spent the night with that gorgeous Geri last night, lucky dog! Mandy's been let down by some bloke who was booked to do some modelling with her and now she wants me to do it. I said yes but I'm not sure. I mean, it's not exactly the most macho way to earn money is it?

Tuesday 11 January 2000 – 9:45pm

Nice timing Mum and Dad. I'm meant to be revising for my mocks and they've decided to go for a formal separation. Great. I suppose it'll be better than them living together here and pretending everything's okay when it isn't, but couldn't they have just hung on till after my exams? Adam and I have made a pact to shoot each other if we ever decide to get married. I don't see why people bother. I mean, why restrict yourself to one person forever when they might turn into a right moose when they hit forty or cheat on you or anything. I can't believe Adam's avoiding Geri, she's a babe. If I know my brother, it can only mean there's someone else on the scene. He doesn't like to have more than one girl on the go at any time, not like my pre-Mandy days! Anyway, I reckon I know who she is – I'd put money on him having a thing with his tutor, Christine, there's definitely something going on there. Well, he deserves it after all that hassle with Kerri. Lucy got let off. It turns out Rob was dousing the bus in petrol trying to trap Lucy and Ruth cos he hated them. What a psycho, I hope no one ever hates me that much.

Thursday 13 January 2000 – 11:43pm

I've been revising. I didn't realize how close my mocks were but they start in a few days. They shouldn't be a problem, though, and anyway, it's not like they're the real thing or anything. I was so right about Adam and his tutor. Apparently, it's been going on for quite a while, he's even written about it in his script for film studies. Yeah, I know, I thought it would be really cheesy too, but it's not, it's really quite good in an *American Pie* kind of way. He's such a jammy git, cos apparently that gorgeous Geri's still after him as well. I don't know what his secret is. I wouldn't tell him that, his head's already huge after bagging a tutor. Mum left Deva today, she thought it was better if she and Dad didn't work together any more now they're separated. And Tony's decided to leave too. He and his girlfriend are going travelling for a year – though only to places where he won't catch any diseases, so that sounds like he really wants to rough it. That means that we all have to take on extra shifts, extra shifts I could do without so close to my mocks. Thanks Mum.

Monday 17 January 2000 – 11:41pm

I messed up my first exam today thanks to Mark and his mates. They were hanging around school this morning. Mark said that just cos the case has been dropped it doesn't mean he's forgotten what I did to him. What's the matter with him? Can't he get it into his thick head that I didn't hurt him on purpose? They hung around outside the window the whole way through my exam, it was impossible to concentrate. Then when I came out, they'd let all the tyres down on the car. I wish he'd just take his mates and naff off, I could really do without all this.

Wednesday 19 January 2000 – 11:45pm

Mandy's just left, I tried to get her to stay the night but she says she thinks I should be preserving my energy for my maths exam tomorrow. I don't need energy to help me pass that, I need a miracle. Anyway, Mandy brought the photos round from that modelling I did for her. She reckons I look gorgeous, but I reckon I just look like a big wuss. Mum's out again with William and Zara's watching some horror movie. I've tried to get her to go to bed and so have Adam and Beth. Oh well, it's up to her if she wants to be knackered tomorrow. I reckon she's only staying up to make sure Mum doesn't try to sneak William in when she gets back.

Thursday 20 January 2000 – 10:56pm

I went over to Mandy's for tea cos her folks were all out. She cooked fish cos it's meant to be good for the brain. Thing was, it was still frozen in the middle – it was gross, like sushi but worse, it made me gag. It was good to get away from home, though, cos Adam and Zara are both giving Mum hell over William. Zara's just being sulky but Adam's really angry cos she hasn't even told Dad she's seeing someone else. I don't know why I'm not bothered, probably cos nothing she does surprises me any more. I mean, poor Dad, he's still convinced that they'll get back together once he's given her a bit of space. He's even asked her to come back and work in Deva again until he finds someone to replace Tony. I hate Mum for putting us all in this position, that we all know something that Dad should know, but at the same time it's not really our place to tell him. I'm not going to, it'd break his heart.

Saturday 22 January 2000 – 9:39pm

Adam's in such a mood, he's been playing his music on full blast for two hours now and just tells us all to get lost when we tell him to turn it down. He's furious with Mum cos he came home from college early and found her here with William, doing it. Can you imagine! He confronted her and told her to tell Dad, which she did, and now Dad's gutted. Beth's staying with him tonight so I'll get the lowdown tomorrow. Still revising, one more exam to go.

Tuesday 25 January 2000 – 11:42pm

Had to help Dad out at Deva tonight cos he was having a Burns' Night party. It was okay to start off with, apart from Dad trying to make me wear a kilt. Dad proceeded to get totally hammered with Ruth and Darren's dad. I had to ring Darren to get him to come and pick Mr O up in the car, he was that smashed. They were so embarrassing, they did a duet of *Donald Where's your Troosers* and then pulled a moony at a load of unsuspecting old grannies on a coach trip.

Friday 27 January 2000 – 11:28pm

Mandy came in to Deva this evening to ask me if I'll do some more modelling for her. I'm tempted cos the money's so good, but I feel such a nancy. She asked about my exams results too, I deliberately hadn't told anyone cos they're so rubbish, but as soon as they heard Mandy ask, Mum and Dad suddenly remembered (a) I'm their son and (b) I've just taken my mocks. I got two Es and a U, so needless to say, none of them were that impressed. I thought I'd finally shaken Mark and his mates, too, but the last couple of days they've been hanging around Deva, making faces at me while I work and that kind of stuff. I can't believe they've got nothing better to do. Why don't they just grow up?

Monday 31 January 2000 – 11:14pm

What a rubbish day. Had a match against King Edwards' after school today and we got annihilated. I don't know what's wrong with me – I missed the easiest of goals, too. It was really embarrassing cos I'd asked Mandy to come and watch and then I played like a giant squid. Mark and his mates were there yet again – can they really have nothing better to do than to stalk me? They started hassling Mandy, so I lost concentration on the game and ended up getting substituted for Noel Mason – I'm miles better than he is. Anyway, I couldn't face watching him screw up the game any more so I went to get changed. Mark and his mates came in and started pushing me about a bit. It was nothing I couldn't handle, but I was pleased when the rest of the team came in and they scarpered, but only after they'd shoved my clothes in the bog though. Mandy got really hacked off with them. She saw they were putting me off my game and had a go at them. I think she thought I'd be pleased, but no way, it's so embarrassing them thinking I have to get my girlfriend to fight my battles. She got in a strop with me and stormed off. I'm getting sick of her moods.

Wednesday 2 February 2000 – 10:48pm

I am so impressed with Adam, he shagged Christine on the kitchen floor in Deva last night. That's what it's all about, loads of exciting sex, not all this sniping at each other like Mum and Dad's garbage. I'm starting to miss my single life, maybe I should get myself out there again. I took Darren with me to football practice tonight, he's thinking of joining the team. We could do with a decent mid-fielder and he's not bad. Mum was out with William again tonight so Zara got her mate Hannah round. Beth was staying with Caroline and Adam had a shift at the pool, so they raided the drinks cabinet, made cocktails and got really trolleyed. So I had to drive Hannah home – it was horrible trying to persuade a drunk thirteen year old, who fancies you, not to throw up in your car. It's all Mum's fault, if she was ever in then none of this junk would be happening.

11:23pm

Made up with Mandy. She says she loves me, feel a bit mean cos I didn't say it back.

Thursday 3 February 2000 – 11:39pm

Mum wants us to meet William – she's invited him round to tea tomorrow afternoon. Beth and Adam have managed to get out of it so I had to promise to be there. I can't wait – not. Zara's got just what she deserves – a great big hangover and Beth and I have been taking great pleasure in playing loud music and doing lots of shouting just to make her feel as bad as she possibly can. Mum's furious with her, cos not only did Hannah's mum have a go at her about being irresponsible, but she got a phone call from an irate woman cos apparently Zara and Hannah had been making nuisance calls last night. Zara's really going off the rails, she told Mum she's a slapper and she hates her. I wonder if Mum still wants William to meet her kids?!

Friday 4 February 2000 – 11:21pm

I played one of Zara's tricks today and skived school. I had to cos Mandy wanted me for this modelling thing she had lined up and I could hardly turn down £100 for a day's work, could I? The tea with William was an absolute disaster. Zara was so rude to him, if it hadn't been so painful it would have been funny. She even asked him if he's shagging Mum – I mean, how do you respond to a thirteen year old asking if you're having sex with her mum? I think we should impose Zara on him a bit more, a few more doses of her and he'll be out of Mum's life for good, won't see him for dust. Adam came home in a right mood, he got sprung by Ruth doing it with Christine in the edit suite at college. Oops!

Wednesday 9 February 2000 – 11:24pm

This thing with Adam and Christine seems pretty serious. I can't believe the way she's stitched him up. He got suspended from college today while they investigate. She is such a cow for saying he attacked her, I mean they're bound to believe her word over his aren't they? I'm really worried for him and I feel like having it out with her myself. I mean, she could ruin his life, he could get chucked out of college for something like this. Even Geri, who was meant to be one of his friends, came into

Deva yesterday and started laying into him. I don't know, sometimes I feel like our family is really dysfunctional – but I guess dysfunctional's normal these days. Speaking of which, Mandy's going to buy a car – have you ever heard anything more ridiculous?! Don't get me wrong, she's my girlfriend and I think she's great, but the girl can't drive. I mean, she nearly killed herself, Mr C and Carol's poodle in one go this afternoon – and that was when someone else had dual control!

Saturday 12 February 2000 – 7:02pm

I can't wait to get out of this dump. I hate school and I hate my family. I'm about to take the most important exams of my life and all everyone can do is yell at me or near me – which ever it is I can't concentrate on learning my periodic table. Adam and Zara are really winding each other up tonight, how come whenever anyone in this family has a problem, she has to pounce on it and go on and on? Lucky I'm getting out of here soon, a group of us are going into town and we're going to try and fix Darren up with one of Polly's mates. I don't think he'll go for her myself, she looks a bit too sweet and innocent for him. *Reminder – remember to get Mandy a Valentine's card.*

Sunday 13 February 2000 – 8:43pm

Last night was really good, just what I needed after all the hassle here. Much to everyone's surprise, Darren did go for Polly's mate Heidi – he said she was really randy as well! I don't know, I think there might be a bit of Darren's bravado and a few lies in there. Mandy got really smashed, I've never seen her so funny. She tried to make the bus driver let her have a go on the way home and got us chucked off, we had to walk the rest of the way. Well, I say walked but Mandy collapsed in a heap when we got to the yard so I had to push her back here in a wheelbarrow – it was hilarious, just this big hysterical bundle of arms and legs. It was a nightmare trying to sneak her up here, Mum was still out on her date with you-know-who, so that was good. But Mandy still managed to wake the others up and now Zara's threatening to tell Mum about it unless I let her have my Travis CD. She can whistle for it, I don't care what she says or what Mum says. Anyway, I got Mandy undressed and into bed and then she decided she fancied a bit of nookie, which was fine by me – it's always fine by me. So there we were, really going for it when Mandy turns green and pukes all over me, it was foul. So then I had to get up in the middle of the night, hose her down and change the sheets. She did tell me she loved me again, which was nice. I haven't said it to her yet, it's not that I don't, cos I do – I think – it's just that the first time I say it I want her to be in a state to remember it.

Monday 14 February 2000 – 11:28pm

I got five Valentine's cards and I only know who sent four of them. I got a home-made one and a serious one from Mandy, one from Zara's mate Hannah, who fancies me, and the usual embarrassment from Mum. I have no idea who sent the other one, though, it was posted in Liverpool – I don't know anyone in Liverpool. Adam had to go before a tribunal hearing at college today – Dad went with him for moral support cos everyone's being off to him. You know, I could kill Ruth, she let someone at the magazine do a story on what's happened and there's this massive mug-shot of Adam on the cover saying 'Sex Pest'. I bet she and her stupid mates feel dead stupid now it's come out Christine was making it all up. She must be seriously warped to have said all that stuff about him, and he nearly got done for it too – it was only at the eleventh hour that a few people spoke up and said they knew they'd been having an affair for ages. Why do women do stuff like that? I mean, especially in her position. It was alright for her to have her naughty little fling, but as soon as she realized her job was in jeopardy, she cried wolf. Why does everyone always presume the man's the one who's lying?

Tuesday 15 February 2000 – 11:12pm

I wish Mandy still lived in her flat, it feels like we never get any time alone. We went back to her place tonight and there was no one in, so we stared to get busy and then Cindy walks in. She offered to go and sit in the conservatory and turn her music up really loud, but it's not really the same. Talk about passion-killer, I feel like I'm about to explode. She's roped me into doing more modelling with her as well. I hate doing it, but I just can't turn that kind of money down. Jez and all the lads gave me hell last week cos one of them found the thermals advert in the *Herald*. They think it's hilarious and keep planting lipsticks and Tampax in my blazer. Now everyone knows about it and one of Sol's mates even asked me to pose nude for his portfolio today – I don't think so.

Thursday 17 February 2000 – 11:16pm

It's good now Darren's joined the football team cos I even get a lift when Adam has the car. It must be ace having a dad who owns a pub, cos not only does he have access to heaps of booze 24/7, but he also gets to use the car every night when his dad's working. We had a pretty good game this afternoon, 2–1 to us. Well, the game was good but the crowd weren't up to much. Mark and his dumb cling-ons turned up calling me pretty boy and stuff like that. I mean, what do they expect me to do, break down crying and beg them to stop? Oh please, do me a large one. Anyway, we were getting changed after the game and they came in and started having a go. So Darren really laid into them, not in an aggressive way, just really witty at their expense. I'm going to be more like that, I'm going to have a think about clever comebacks. I hadn't really thought about it before, but they're such a thick load of gimps, it's easy to get under their skin just by being more intelligent – which isn't hard. I mean, anyone will get slaughtered in a fight when it's three against one, but if the fight was with words and not fists, I'd be laughing.

Sunday 20 February 2000 – 11:47pm

I was really glad to be on half term until Mum and Dad had a massive argument and, guess what, Zara started it – for a change. I'm sure she stirs up trouble on purpose, she's got such a sick sense of humour – she just thrives on chaos. It all started when Mum and William went out to the opera last night. Beth was staying with Sally, I was out with Mandy and Adam was at Cream with Geri. Zara was obviously in a huff cos she was in on her own, so she wandered off to Deva and told Dad Mum's been neglecting us. I don't agree with most of what Mum does, but she doesn't neglect us – she's always on at me about something.

Wednesday 24 February 2000 – 11:22pm

Training was rubbish today. Darren couldn't make it cos he's got to work in The Dog to get some money together for his car insurance or something like that. I tested out his theory on Mark, though, and thought it had worked to start off with. He and his mates were messing about on the sidelines, trying to distract me by shouting out stuff about Mandy and all that during the game. I deliberately didn't give them a rise, in fact I pretended I hadn't even noticed they were there. They were pretty hacked off by the end of the game so they flushed what they thought were my clothes down the bog. Turns out they were Gripper's – he went mad. I was chuffed cos I thought I'd got one over on them, but then I went to the car to come home and they'd nicked two of the wheels. This whole hate campaign is getting ridiculous now, it's not even funny. I had to get the car towed to a garage, which cost me forty quid I haven't got. When Adam finds out he's going to kill me, not to mention Dad. I'll have to make something up. I can't tell him the truth, I mean, it sounds so pathetic to say, 'Daddy, these three bullies stole me wheels, boo hoo.' Next time I see Mark I'm going to kill him – one on one, just me and him, then we'll see how tough he really is without his lynch-mob to help him out. Stupid prat.

Sunday 27 February 2000 – 11:21pm

Adam's being so tight about the car. He reckons I'm not responsible enough to take care of it and shouldn't be allowed to use it any more cos he never had his own car when he was seventeen. He told Dad and, as I thought, he went mental. He paid for new wheels and I have to work in Deva every day after school for two weeks to pay him back. Great, it's not as if I've got physics coursework to hand in in the morning or anything. I'm going to be up all night at this rate.

Wednesday 1 March 2000 – 12:45am

I'm done in, had to work all night in Deva again and missed football. Darren called in on his way back and said I didn't miss much, we lost. See, Dad making me miss a match is having a detrimental effect, they just can't do without me. When Darren had gone it was pretty quiet, so I got on with a bit of homework, or at least I tried to. I got another visit from Mark and co. I wish they'd just get lost, I mean, what do they want from me – blood? They made a right mess of the place, throwing food around and knocking chairs over like a load of kids. That's why I got back here so late, cos I had to clean it all up. I really hate Mark, he just doesn't give up. When I see him on his own he's going to be so sorry.

Sunday 5 March 2000 – 8:43pm

Darren's started hanging around with Mark and his two gimps – he reckons they're alright. Yeah right. They all came in to Deva and were having a laugh – Mark made this big show of apologizing to me about all the stuff he and his mates have been doing. He said no hard feelings and we shook hands, but I still don't trust him. He's a moron. Mandy came in, too, and sat with them, I'm sure Mark fancies her cos he was really flirting – I bet he was just doing it to wind me up. Friends with him? My arse. Mandy's on my case as well, she was moaning that we haven't done it for ages today. I can't believe her, she's the one who moved out of her own flat into a madhouse. And anyway, for the first time ever, I just don't really feel like it at the moment. I'm so stressed out, it must be the exam pressure building up or something like that.

Tuesday 7 March 2000 – 11:40pm

I can't wait till this working in Deva in the evenings malarkey is over and I can have a life again. I don't like it that Mandy's started hanging around with Darren and Mark, and his two pikey mates Kenny and Steve. I think she's trying to make me jealous cos we haven't been getting on that well for a while. Oh well, it's not for much longer. Mum and Dad found out Beth has been saying she's at Sally's and vice versa when really they've been going clubbing. It's her turn to spend her evenings in Deva now. I hope Mark and co don't give her any hassle, though, cos I know they fancy her, they used to shout about shagging her to put me off at football.

Wednesday 8 March 2000 – 11:45pm

I love the internet. Adam just told me about this site called Geri.Cam. One of Adam's college mates put a web-cam in Geri's bedroom in halls and it goes out live – it's brilliant. We just watched her take her tash off with wax – that has got to hurt, it looked like she was whipping a plaster off her lip. Then we watched her getting undressed – man she has got an incredible body, I was practically drooling until she farted. I didn't know girls did that – apart from Beth and Zara, but they don't count. Mandy's never done it in front of me, but I don't think I could fancy her any more if she suddenly let rip. By the way, she bought herself a car today. She hasn't passed her test yet, she just thought it looked nice. Girls' logic.

Thursday 9 March 2000 – 11:21pm

Had a great night last night. It sounds really sad, but me

and Mandy went to the quiz night at The Dog. It was a right laugh cos Darren got us free drinks all night and we won. At first Darren wanted me and Mandy to be on his team with Mark, Kenny and Steve – but Mandy's sick of them messing about and making sexual innuendoes all the time and she said she just wanted to be on a team with me. Darren is so sore he lost, I don't think he realized how thick Mark and his mates are – he reckons if they had one brain cell between them it would die of loneliness. Some of the stuff they shouted out was laughable – even Beth's more intelligent than they are – and she's dumb. Mandy got a bit narked with me cos I really lorded it over them about winning, but they deserved to have their noses rubbed in it after all the junk they've done to me. She reckons we should just bury the hatchet once and for all. She's so girly and romanticized sometimes, just cos girls can have bitch fights one day and be best mates the next doesn't mean it'll work for me.

Sunday 12 March 2000 – 9:19pm

Mandy and I went to our usual spot in Delamere Forest again today. It started to rain as soon as we got there so we sat in the car and talked and snogged and had an excellent shag. I finally told her I love her and guess what she did? She cried. Why do girls have to do that, it's not that big a deal. Anyway, we've decided we're going to save up and go on holiday to Tenerife after exams. Jez's folks have got a place out there and there's a whole gang going. I might even see if there are any single girls who we can fix Darren up with, I bet he'd love to come. I'll ask him tomorrow at football, it's a big match then we're all going out afterwards to get hammered. I let Mandy drive part of the way back cos she's got her test on Friday – never again, I was scared for my life. She doesn't so much park as land.

Reminder – must remember to have some conciliatory chocolate at the ready on Friday.

Thursday 16 March 2000 – 8:45am

BASTARD

He's going to pay for this. I'm going to kill him, I swear it. I can't get me head round what's happened. Is this for real?

10:32am

I've had a shower, but I still feel dirty. I can smell his sweat on me. I feel sick. I can't sleep cos every little noise has got me jumping out of my skin. I've turned into a stupid, snivelling wimp overnight. I can't even get comfortable cos I'm so sore and I'm still bleeding. I don't know what to do, I can't go to the doctor, not about that.

7:32pm

Mandy came round earlier to have a go at me for not

turning up last night. It was weird, I could see her mouth moving, but everything she said sounded jumbled and loud, really loud. She thinks I've lost interest in her and that I've got someone else, I didn't know what to say so I didn't say anything. I think she thought I was upset by what she said so she apologised and tried to kiss me. I wanted to kiss her back, I really did, but my mind was playing tricks on me and every time my lips touched hers I imagined I was kissing Gibbs. I recoiled away from her, I had to. Mandy got really upset, and started crying. I know I should have reached out to her and hugged her, but I couldn't, just the thought of being intimate with someone, anyone, even my own girlfriend makes me feel sick. She tried to get me to talk about what's bugging me, but I don't want to hear my own voice let alone hers whining on at me. She left in a huff. I know I could lose her if I don't sort things out, but I just can't cope with anyone being in my face at the moment. Mum and Zara are having a screaming row downstairs, I don't know what it's about, I don't even care, I just wish they'd shut up. I can't cope with all this noise.

Friday 17 March 2000 – 4:04am

I wish I could sleep, then at least I could forget for a few hours. My head's spinning and my heart's beating so fast I feel lightheaded. I'm exhausted and I want to sleep, but every time I close my eyes I see him – standing over me, smirking. I've never hated anybody as much as I *hate* him.

4:33am

Still can't sleep. Keep crying all the time. What's happening to me?

5:37am

A few days ago I was happy, it's so recent, but I can't remember how it feels. I can't believe it's all ruined now, I don't care about anything any more, not Mandy, not football, nothing. I just want to sleep and I can't. I just want this nightmare to go away, but it won't. When I think about it I realize I could have done so much more to prevent him doing what he did. If I hadn't phoned Adam to tell him about my goal, then I wouldn't have been the last one in the changing rooms. If Darren had just waited for me and been there when they came looking for me, then this would never have happened. I feel so stupid for not realizing what was going on. Even when the others were holding me down and he was tugging at my trousers, it still didn't cross my mind that he was going to do that. I thought they were going to nick my clothes or something and leave me naked in the middle of nowhere. That I could have handled, but this? I just want to die. I wish he'd killed me, then I wouldn't have to live with it. What kind of psycho does something like that?

7:12am

I can't stop thinking about what happened. I've been awake all night, replaying it in my mind, wondering if I could have done more to protect myself. I suppose it all started to go wrong after the match. I scored the winning goal and Gibbs was really hacked off that we beat his team. He came looking for me with Kenny and Steve in the changing rooms when everyone else had gone. He started emptying my kit bag and smashing all my stuff up. I was more annoyed than scared cos I knew I couldn't take on all three of them. I tried to ignore them and hoped they'd get bored if I didn't react, but now I think their intention was to do whatever it took to make me react. They beat me up pretty badly, and Gibbs peed all over my clothes. I thought that would be it, but then they dragged me into the bogs and gave me a head-flush. Luckily that old caretaker, Jabba, must have heard something cos he came in and they legged it. That should have been the end of it, I should have just got away from them when I had the chance, but I didn't. When I got to the car park they were sitting in their car laughing. I saw red. I went over and grabbed Gibbs and slammed the car door on his leg as hard as I could. I wanted to break it, I wanted to kill him. I got in my car and drove off as fast as I could. I was pretty scared cos I knew they were chasing me and our car can only do seventy at a push. Eventually I lost them and I started to make my way home, when I got caught at a level crossing. Suddenly they appeared from nowhere and smashed into the back of me. I almost lost control of the car. I managed to lose them again by cutting through a field on a mud track but my wheels got stuck and the car wouldn't move. I flooded the engine by trying to get it out, I was revving like a madman cos I could see their headlights getting closer in the rear-view mirror. I had to run for it, I didn't have a choice. They caught up with me and dragged me to the floor, taking it in turns to kick and punch me. I begged them to stop, but they were like a pack of dogs – I thought they were going to kill me. Gibbs sat on my chest calling me gay boy and faggot. I couldn't breathe and the only thing I could do to get him off me was to spit in his face. That was like signing my own death warrant. He went ballistic hitting me so hard my nose and mouth were streaming with blood. He got Kenny and Mark to pin me to the bonnet of the car face down and that's when he did it. I can't remember how long it lasted, all I can remember is the pain. If I'd have known what he was capable of I would have walked away when I had the chance. I wish I'd never provoked him.

10:20pm

I didn't go into school today. I told Mum I was revising at home and luckily she fell for it. I feel like I never want to go to school again. I don't want to face anyone. At least Mum and Dad are far too busy yelling at Zara to notice that there's anything up with me. I feel like what's happened is written all over my face and people will know when they see me, but no one's said anything so far. I've started to dread going to bed, cos I know I won't sleep and there's just hours of solitude ahead of me, when all I can think about is what happened.

Saturday 18 March 2000 – 4:14pm

I didn't get any sleep again last night. I knew that would happen. I probably look terrible, I know I feel it. I have to pretend that everything's okay and act normal in front of the family. I couldn't bear it if they found out. What would they think of me?

Sunday 19 March 2000 – 3:17am

Can't sleep. Blackness. Nothing but this heavy, sagging misery hanging over me. Can't do anything but lie here. My mind won't let my body sleep and my body won't let me forget what's happened. Every part of me feels bruised and broken. Why did it happen? Does it mean I'm gay?

6:01am

I feel like I'm never going to be able to sleep again cos every time I try I can feel him on top of me, slamming my face down on the car and holding me by the hair. I can taste my own blood in my mouth. I can feel him pushing himself inside me, I can hear myself screaming for him to stop, but he's not listening, none of them are listening. Why did I let him do that to me? I should have fought harder.

Monday 20 March 2000 – 8:12pm

I feel knackered, I didn't get much sleep cos of the nightmares. I keep waking myself up crying and I don't even know I'm doing it. I hope no one's heard me. I feel like I'm out of control. A week ago everything was fine and now suddenly I've lost it. My life is spinning into chaos and there's nothing I can do. I don't even know who I am any more, it's almost like Gibbs killed the real me and now I'm just – I don't know what I am or why I'm even bothering to try and make sense of all this, I can't make sense of anything. I didn't go to school today cos I'm so tired – it's good Mum and Dad think I'm revising cos it gets them off my case. I just lay on my bed all day staring at the ceiling, most of the time my mind's blank, like it's shut down or something. I've got no energy. I can't face doing anything or seeing anyone, I just feel numb.

Tuesday 21 March 2000 – 10:00am

I think Mum knows there's something up with me cos she's being extra nice. She keeps asking me what's wrong, but how can I tell her? I mean, I don't even know if there's a word or a phrase for what he did to me. I know it's not rape cos men don't get raped.

3:21pm

I feel so alone. Has this ever happened to anyone else? Has Gibbs done it to anyone else? Am I being a big wuss by letting it affect me this much? Maybe it happens all the time and other blokes just take it in their stride and get on with it. I hate myself for letting it happen. What kind of man am I if I can't even look after myself? I despise myself almost as much as I despise *him*.

Wednesday 22 March 2000 – 3:22pm

I'm getting used to having no sleep, but I hate having so

much time to think about stuff. I've got pretty used to all the noises this house makes at night and don't get as freaked out by it as I did at first. This room has become my sanctuary and prison at the same time. I want to get out there and just be normal again, but I can't. Here is the only place I feel safe. The family's just starting to notice there's something up and keep asking what's wrong. I've fobbed them off with exam stress so far, but I'm not sure how long they'll go with it. Hopefully, it will be long enough for me to get my head together.

4:52pm

I feel like someone's grabbed my whole life and thrown it up in the air like a big pile of paper and now I'm just scattered all over the place, trampled. I didn't even know Gibbs was gay until he attacked me. Somehow he doesn't seem the type. Maybe he's right about me, maybe cos he is, he can tell whether other blokes are. I never even considered that I could be, but maybe I am. I don't feel like I am, but the night he attacked me, when he was actually doing it, I got hard. I'm disgusted with myself, I don't know why it happened. Maybe I'm a sick, warped pervert like he is. Maybe I deserved it. It's not that I enjoyed it or wanted him to do it, I didn't. I could hear myself screaming at him to stop, I was willing it not to happen but it was like I lost control. My mind was saying no but my body was saying yes. But they were holding me down. There was nothing I could do.

5:30pm

Mandy came over just now, she wants to patch things up. I'm deliberately distancing myself from her cos I can't cope with anything too heavy at the moment. I know I'm hurting her feelings, but I can't see any other way. I have to deal with this on my own cos no one's going to understand. I just sat there and listened to her talk. She was pleading with me to tell her what she did wrong – as if she could ever do anything to offend me. She was begging me to get back with her. It was weird cos I was aching to hold her, I just wanted to bury my face in her hair and breathe her in and feel how I used to feel. I wish I could tell her what's happened. I couldn't even have her touch me without flinching. She thinks I didn't say anything cos I hate her. I wish she knew it was cos I had such a big lump in my throat, I would have cried if I'd have tried to speak. And I wouldn't have been able to stop myself telling her all about it. Then what would she have thought of me? Her boyfriend's a big, gay cry baby. It's better this way.

11:20pm

Mum reckons I'm going to burn myself out cos I'm doing so much revision – if only she knew. I keep thinking about Mandy, I really miss her. Maybe she would understand if I told her, I mean she had all that junk with her dad – she might even be able to help. The thing is, it could go either way. She could be totally great and supportive about it or she could totally freak out. At the moment I'd rather keep her at arm's length than risk losing her for ever.

Thursday 23 March 2000 – 6:40pm

I had to get out of the house this afternoon, there's hell

at home. Zara skived school yesterday with one of her mates and got drunk. As usual Mum and Dad are screaming at each other and not her. Ever since you-know-what, it feels like someone's turned the volume up on the whole world. Any kind of noise drives me mad and gives me a massive headache. I went for a walk and I feel a bit better for getting out. I was like Forrest Gump though, I just kept on and on walking, like I couldn't stop. I hadn't planned where I was going, but I ended up at this place we used to go to when we were kids in Chester Meadows. I hadn't been there for years but it felt like yesterday. It's like a copse on the bank of the river, but it's kind of swampy too. There's this massive, old tree that hangs across the Dee and we used to have a blue, nylon rope with loads of knots on it that we used to use to swing from one bank to the other. It's gone now. I wandered around for a while, thinking about when we were kids and wondering if I'll ever have that innocent kind of happiness again. I felt safe there, I think I might have even forgotten what's happened, momentarily. I bumped into Mandy on the way back. She was on a driving lesson and just stopped the car in the middle of the road. She wants me to do some more modelling with her. I just wanted her to leave me alone so I agreed to it, even though I've got no intention of going. I know I'm being a git to her, but if I'd have tried to back out of it she'd have given me hell and I can't cope with that, not now. Anyway, she'll know by now that I'm not going to show – I feel bad, but she'll get over it.

8:30pm

Mandy's just dumped me. She came round just now, furious cos I didn't show for the shoot. I told her I forgot. She still thinks I've got someone else. I wish I could explain that I just need some time on my own to sort myself out. Maybe it's for the best. We'll get back together in a few weeks, when all this is over.

Friday 24 March 2000 – 2:07am

Can't sleep cos I woke myself up screaming. I've been with Mandy when she's had nightmares about her Dad before. I never thought it would happen to me. I went downstairs for a while to watch some telly and ended up watching some American chat show. It was crazy, I had to turn the volume down cos they were all yelling at each other and trying to punch each other. It made me feel really nervous, I was just about to switch over when they did this item on rape. The presenter defined rape as non-consensual sex between a man and a woman, a man and a man or a woman and a woman. So men do get raped? Is that what happened to me?

4:34am

I can't stop thinking about that TV programme, it's made me feel panicky. My heart's racing, my mouth's dry, I feel sick, I'm all sweaty and my stomach is killing me. I keep having to rush to the loo. What's happening to me? Ever since the beating, I feel constantly surprised by how my body reacts to things.

5:12am

Rape is such a huge serious thing, that can't be what

happened to me, can it? I mean, I always thought rape meant a man forcing himself on a woman, I've never even heard of it happening to blokes and it certainly doesn't make me feel any better if that is what it was. Women are weaker than men and that's why they get overpowered, but there's no reason why it should have happened to me. I feel like a freak.

7:30pm

Jez just called to see if I want to go out tonight. I tried to sound normal and told him I have to work in Deva – but I don't really, I just can't face going into town with a pack of blokes. I know it's irrational, but I resent Jez at the moment. He's had such a charmed life, his parents are loaded and they still love each other, things are going great with Polly and he's got a place at Manchester next year. What have I got? A family that hates each other and a big, dark secret.

Sunday 26 March 2000 – 4:40pm

I'm getting quite good at hiding my secret. Most of the time I just sit here in a kind of numb cocoon, not really thinking about the beating – not really thinking about anything – I've just trained my mind to go blank when it all gets too much. I've learnt to constantly have one of my school books at hand so if any of the family walk in it looks like I'm revising. I'm sick of them asking me if I'm okay. I'm fine, I just want to be left alone. I just want to forget about it.

Monday 27 March 2000 – 8:30pm

If I had my way, I wouldn't even go downstairs for family meals, I can't hack them all giving me concerned looks as if I'm some kind of freak. Mandy came over earlier to get some of her stuff. It felt so final, like we really are splitting up. I suppose I hadn't really believed that this could be it for us until tonight. A voice inside of me was calling her back as she left, but I just couldn't find the words. I just watched her go like the stupid jerk I am. She still thinks I'm seeing someone else, I haven't got the energy to argue. Part of me's annoyed that she could think that of me, but part of me is relieved she has an answer to all this in her head already – at least she won't start asking more questions.

9:02pm

I hate Gibbs so much for what he's done to me. I feel like I'm never going to be normal again. I really wish I had someone to talk to. I got a number for the Samaritans out of the phone book just now – 0345 90 90 90 – they'll probably think I'm some kid messing about if they hear a male voice say, 'I think I've been raped.' Who's going to take me seriously? The thing is, that I can feel myself sinking and I think I do need help, I keep having really bad thoughts. I don't want to go on if it's going to be like this forever. What's the point?

9:40pm

I'd psyched myself up to ring the helpline on my mobile, when Dad knocked on my door. I was half relieved to see him, for a split second I felt like bursting into tears and telling him everything, but when I looked at his face he looked like he knew and he despised me for it. He asked me to go downstairs where there was a policeman waiting for me. My stomach lurched and I was terrified I was going to get arrested for under-age, gay sex. Apparently, there's CCTV footage of me filling the car up with petrol and not paying for it on the night of the beating. I almost laughed, I mean, in the grand scale of things, who gives a toss? I don't. I had to endure a lecture from Dad – he reckons I was drinking and driving. He's disappointed in me, but not as much as he would be if he knew the truth. He's forbidden me from driving the car for three months cos I'm irresponsible. Nothing surprises me any more, it's not as if my life could get any worse.

Tuesday 28 March 2000 – 5:43pm

I went back into school today and it was a nightmare. I feel like I have nothing in common with my friends any more. I really need to talk to someone, but if I told Jez something like this he'd run a mile. I would too, if one of my friends told me they'd been raped. I'd think they were having a laugh or they were gay. Do you think you can subconsciously give off gay vibes?

Wednesday 29 March 2000 – 10:12pm

Darren came round tonight, he was on his way to football and asked me if I wanted a lift. I told him I can't play any more till after my exams – he seemed surprised but swallowed it. He can't understand why me and Mandy split up, he thinks I'm mad. I had a bit of a go at him and I think he thinks I'm a nutter. I don't care, I don't need him.

Saturday 1 April 2000 – 12:32am

I can't sleep. Mum and William have just got home from the theatre and gone to bed. I can't get the visual images of what they're doing out of my head. I feel sick, I'm such a freak thinking about my own mother having sex. What's wrong with me? I've got to get out of here, I'm going for a walk.

3:19pm

I went back to Chester Meadows last night. It took me hours to get there and it was so dark. Normally I would have been pretty spooked by being out there in the middle of the night, but I wasn't scared. It was weird cos I was in the middle of nowhere in the dead of night and it's a pretty eerie place, but I just didn't care. I guess once you've been raped then there's nothing worse that can happen to you. I don't care if anything did happen – maybe it would be better for everyone if I wasn't around any more.

Sunday 2 April 2000 – 2:00am

I've just been on the internet to try and get some more information. I typed in rape and there were 37,050 sites.

Then I typed in male rape and there were 226. That sums it up really, I'm even a minority in a minority group – no wonder I feel like a freak. Mum definitely knows there's something wrong cos it's the first time I've ever remembered Mothers' Day. She thinks it's to do with me and Mandy splitting up, everyone does. I think I might tell her, I'm not sure though. I mean, it's a pretty huge thing to dump on her and she can't just say, 'There, there,' and it'll all go away. She'd be gutted for me – maybe I should just keep it to myself.

9:30pm

One of these days I'm going to kill Zara. She's such a spoilt, malicious little cow. She seems oblivious to anyone's feelings but her own, but as soon as she's a bit down in the dumps then we all know about it. Tonight she had her stupid friend Steph round and they got all hysterical and screechy cos they were watching horror videos. They thought it would be really hilarious to pretend there was a phone call for me so they could get into my room and have a snoop around. I was terrified it would be Gibbs on the phone, really scared, so I went mad when I realized it was all a hoax. I grabbed Zara and shook her and yelled at her and Mum and William had to pull me off. Zara started to blub and of course I got it in the neck, but she asked for it. That's the problem with her, Mum and Dad are far too soft on her, she gets away with murder. Mum keeps knocking on the door and yelling at me about Zara, she called me a bully, she just doesn't get it, does she?

Monday 3 April 2000 – 8:40pm

I thought Darren was my mate. He came round earlier, I thought it was cos I haven't seen him for a while, but he just wanted to sound me out about Mandy. He's interested in her and asked if I minded them getting together. Of course I mind, I love her and she loves me, but I couldn't say that to Darren. I know I've treated her badly, but I didn't have a choice. I started to tell Darren that I never wanted to break up with Mandy and he just looked at me like I was crazy. I knew he wouldn't understand. I can't believe he's sniffing around her already – mates just don't do that, I thought it was like an unspoken rule or something.

Tuesday 4 April 2000 – 5:34am

I keep having this recurring dream that I'm running through Delamere Forest and there's this car chasing me with Gibbs at the wheel. I get to the place where me and Mandy used to go, and there's Darren on top of her, doing it from behind and they're both laughing at me. Then I realize that the car has caught up with me, and Gibbs gets out but he's massive, he's about ten feet tall and he's playing with himself and he says it's his turn when Darren's finished. I try to get him to leave her alone, but I can't, he's too strong for me, so I start to cry and beg him not to, but he just pushes me aside and gets on with it. Each time I wake myself up, screaming and panting, his face fresh in my mind. Will I ever be able to sleep properly again?

Friday 7 April 2000 – 11:31pm

Adam's gone skiing with some of his college mates and I've been roped into working in Deva. I tried to get out of it saying I've got loads of revision to do, but Mum and Dad think that's what I've been doing locked away in my room for the past few weeks, so they reckon I can afford to take some time off. It's tough having to act normal when all I want to do is crawl into my bed and never come out. I'm terrified of Gibbs and his mates coming in and smashing me up again. I don't know what I'd do if I saw him now. I don't even want to think about it.

Saturday 8 April 2000 – 11:21pm

Mandy and Darren came in to Deva tonight, obviously on a date. I can't believe she's going out with him, she knows what he's like with girls. How could she could get over me so quickly? It was horrible watching them together, holding hands and kissing, I felt like someone was sticking their hand down my throat and ripping my guts up. Mandy kept looking over at me – I think she wanted to make sure I saw. She wants to hurt me back and I can't blame her for that after what I've done to her. She could hurt me any other way, but why does she have to do it with him?

Monday 10 April 2000 – 11:16pm

Things are getting really stressful at school with the

exams coming up. I keep trying to forget about what's happened and do some revision, but I just don't get it. I'm having real trouble with chemistry, I just can't remember any of the basic stuff, let alone how to manufacture sulphuric acid from sulphur. Ever since the beating, I've managed to get out of games. I get really panicky around groups of lads, when they're getting all raucous. I tried to get out of it today, but Mr Tucker had a go at me for skiving and ordered me to get changed. There's something about other people's aggression these days that just makes me want out. I legged it out of school and went to Chester Meadows for the afternoon. I couldn't go home, cos I knew school would be ringing.

Wednesday 12 April 2000 – 9:15pm

I couldn't face school today cos I knew Mr Tucker would be after me about Monday. I went for a walk along the river and bumped into Cindy. She seems to think that just cos she's Mandy's mate she has the God-given right to stick her nose into my business. She was trying to get me to confide in her about why me and Mandy finished – as if I'd tell her! When I made it clear I wasn't up for a deep and meaningful chat with her, she got really stroppy with me and told me dumping me was the best thing Mandy ever did. Cheers, now I feel better – not.

Thursday 13 April 2000 – 1:56am

Can't sleep. I saw Gibbs today. I was walking over the

bridge when he and Kenny and Steve appeared from nowhere. I just froze. They surrounded me and pushed me about a bit and I couldn't even speak let alone fight back. Luckily, there were a few people around, so they left me alone after that. But I couldn't move from the bridge for almost two hours, I felt like I was stuck. I wish I knew what's happening to me. I never would have let anyone push me around like that before. I just don't get how he could have done that to me, in front of two other people as well. How can he go round thinking that's normal? Has he done it to anyone else? It makes me mad with myself that I'm such a weed these days. Perhaps he can forget about it and laugh it off with his mates. But the more time goes by the more I feel that this is something I'm going to have to live with for the rest of my life.

10:14pm

I've got to get away from Zara, she's really winding me up at the moment. She's the only person who can get to me and make me totally lose my rag. I used to be able to ignore her, but now I just want to kill her. She was going on at me being weird this morning and she said Mandy dumped me cos she wanted to go out with a real man. I don't know what happened, I just went for her and I don't know what would have happened if Beth hadn't split us up. Then Mum walked in and had a big go at me – how come no one ever has a go at Zara about the way she speaks to people? She reckons I should go easy on her cos she's having a tough time at school at the moment – she's having a tough time! What about me?

Sunday 16 April 2000 – 9:12am

I had that dream again last night and I can't stop crying. It feels weird, I don't want to be a baby about all of this but I just can't control myself, it's like this great big wave of emotion keeps coming over me and knocking me over every time I think I'm okay.

Tuesday 18 April 2000 – 8:20pm

I nearly told Mum today. She knows something's going on and I think she realizes it's not just splitting up with Mandy. She said she's really worried about me cos I'm withdrawn and moody at the moment. She asked me to tell her what was up, she said she and Dad will love me whatever. I wonder if she'd really think that if she knew? Just as I was about to tell her, the phone rang and she had to dash off to see Zara's headmaster. It's like she has a radar to cause trouble when one of us is getting a bit of attention from Mum and Dad. While everyone was out I found a number of a helpline that's just for blokes. It's called Survivors – 020 7833 3737. I haven't called it yet, though I've been pretty close to doing so, but I think I'm going to. The amount of times I've tried and then lost my nerve and put the phone down. I just don't feel I can say it to anyone, I don't want to be judged. I feel ashamed I have to seek help for something I could have prevented.

9:14pm

I think it might be easier to tell someone I know. I can't

tell Mum and Dad cos they're so wrapped up with Zara, Adam's still away skiing and Jez would be really freaked out. I wish I hadn't hurt Mandy so much, I'm sure she could help, she's been there. I'm not sure if she'll take my call though, and I don't blame her. I suppose there's only one way to find out, I've already lost everything there is to lose. Here goes.

9:20pm

Her mobile was turned off. What do I do now? I'm going to have to try Survivors.

9:40pm

I just spoke to a bloke at Survivors. It wasn't as bad as I thought and he advised me to go to the police if I feel able, get medical checks and tell someone. He said I shouldn't be going through this alone. I feel better for calling, but also scared. I never thought about it before, but what if I caught something from him. What if I've got HIV? This whole thing keeps on getting worse – just when I think I've reached rock bottom, I sink even lower.

Wednesday 19 April 2000 – 4:38am

Haven't been to sleep yet, too much going on in my head. I went on the internet and found out some stuff about HIV. I wish I hadn't now. I may not live to see my twenty-first, I might never see all those countries I haven't been to. I'm meant to outlive my parents, not the other way round. I can see them all at my funeral now, I can see my coffin, I can see them all crying – even Zara. Why did this happen to me? I'm just a kid.

Thursday 20 April 2000 – 10:34am

There's loads of screaming going on downstairs. Zara's really done it this time, she only torched her school. She is such a psycho, I feel really weird towards her at the moment. I mean I love her cos I have to and all that, but she makes it so difficult to like her. I hate the way she manipulates and bullies people, I hate that unpredictable vicious streak in her. Sometimes she reminds me of Gibbs. If she can torch her school, then what else is she capable of?

Friday 21 April 2000 – 9:20pm

Zara's been suspended for a month. Great, that means she'll be hanging around the house poking her nose in where it's not wanted. I wonder why she's always in trouble. I mean, we live in a nice big house, she gets anything she asks for, she's got loads of mates – so how come she's such a nightmare? I know it's tough on her with everything that's been going on with Mum and Dad – but she acts like she's the only one who's affected by it. I don't know, maybe I shouldn't be so hard on her I mean, there might be something going on with her that I don't know about. I should have a talk with her, but she's so hostile and I know I'll end up getting angry with her and flying off the handle.

Easter Sunday 23 April 2000 – 5:50pm

Mum and Dad bought me some new football boots for Easter, that shows how much attention they pay me cos I've barely been out of the house for the past five weeks, let alone play football. I started to get all lethargic so I've nicked Adam's weights out of his room. Seeing Gibbs the other day made me determined that something like that will never happen to me again. I hate feeling like a weed, like I can't take care of myself.

8:05pm

Dad just came in to see me. He wanted advice on Zara – how come they only ever want to talk about her? The rest of us need them as well, okay, maybe not Adam, he's pretty sorted, but I do and Beth does. I mean, it wasn't so long ago that the bloke she was engaged to got killed in a really horrific way. They think that just cos she doesn't talk about it that she's okay, but she's not. She tries to be brave cos she doesn't want to burden them, but she really is quite screwed up about men after him. I hate the way Mum and Dad think that cos they spend so much time dealing with Zara, they fill their quota for parental worry and the rest of us are okay.

11:32pm

I've just been for a walk. I bumped into Mandy and I tried to get her to go for a drink with me but she told me to get lost. I wish I'd told her right from the start, I hate this feeling that she's slipping away from me. I tried to explain why I've been so weird recently, I asked her if she was like this after her dad raped her. I thought she might realize what I was trying to say, I thought she'd make everything okay. How wrong could I be – she was insulted that I thought anything I was going through could possibly be as bad as all that junk with her Dad. I really, really offended her – of course what happened to her was miles worse than this, I just thought she might understand. I don't think I could tell her now, she'd think I was making it up to try and get her back. I hate the thought of her with Darren and I hate the way she looks at me, she's so cold towards me these days. I don't think things can ever be the same again between us. I've lost her haven't I? I wish I could rewind to this time last year when all I was worried about was how many Easter eggs I was going to get.

Tuesday 25 April 2000 – 4:53am

I had that dream again and now I'm too hyper to go back to sleep. I went for a drink with Adam tonight. He reckons he knows what I'm going through – I don't think. Then he gave me this whole spiel about Mandy and there being more fish in the sea. I'm sick of people assuming it's about her. I mean, yeah, I'm gutted we split up and all that, but that's just the tip of the iceberg. When I told him it wasn't Mandy, he started another lecture on 'A' levels not being everything. I'm insulted he thinks I'm such a wuss that I'd let my exams get to me this much.

Thursday 27 April 2000 – 6:56pm

Adam says he had a chat with Mandy yesterday. He reckons she doesn't hate me but she's very confused about what went wrong with us. That's it, she's too important to lose. I'm going to tell her.

Friday 28 April 2000 – 6:32am

I went round to Mandy's last night and she wasn't in – her mum said she was out with Darren. She invited me in for a cup of tea. It felt weird being there without Mandy, knowing she wouldn't want me to be there. I had a bit of a chat with Mrs C, she's really nice. She says she thinks it's a shame me and Mandy split up, she thought we were well suited. I told her that I really care about Mandy and I'm hoping the split isn't permanent. She looked at me like she felt sorry for me. She knows Mandy's moved on. I felt really comfortable talking to her, she just seemed like she had time for me. I think I might have confided in her. I know there's not much that can shock her about blokes like Gibbs after being married to Mandy's dad for however long they were married. I wonder if he ever did anything like that to her? It's weird isn't it, I mean, can you ever know another person, I mean really know them and everything that's happened to them? I'm sure I would have told her if we hadn't been interrupted. Ruth had come round to see the baby. I stayed for a few minutes while she was there. I can't be gay can I, cos I still find her attractive? A year ago I was so sure I could get her into bed any time I wanted, now I'm not even sure who I am. I'm not sure if I want to be alive.

Saturday 29 April 2000 – 11:23pm

Spent all night lying awake thinking of Mandy. I couldn't get her out of my head, just knowing she was out there with Darren, wondering if she has a better time with him than she had with me. Wondering if she's told him she loves him. Wondering if she's seen him naked, making myself feel sick by thinking about them doing it. I went round to her place first thing this morning. I really wanted her to understand that I never meant to hurt her. She was really distant towards me, I could tell she felt really uncomfortable with me. It makes me so sad when I think of all the laughs we used to have and now it has to be like this. I tried to tell her what Darren's like, that all he want is to get his leg over and then he won't want to know her. She refused to listen and tried to walk away. I begged her not to sleep with him, she slapped me round the face and told me it's none of my business. What have I done?

Sunday 30 April 2000 – 7:12pm

I've been trying to get hold of Mandy all day. I just need to explain, but she won't take any of my calls. I've tried sending her text messages, too, but she won't reply. She won't even let me apologize. I know I was out of order saying what I said, but it's only cos I care. She deserves more than to be one of Darren's conquests.

11:30pm

I feel like I just want to curl up and die. When I went downstairs Mum said there was a message on the answerphone for me. It was Mandy, she told me to stop trying to contact her cos she doesn't want to speak to me. Then there was Darren's voice saying Mandy's with him now and she doesn't need me chasing her. Beth and Zara heard it and now they probably think I'm a mad stalker. The thing that guts me the most is that they had obviously had a conversation about me, like I'm some kind of deranged pest.

Tuesday 2 May 2000 – 10:17pm

I walked out of my chemistry exam this afternoon. Why mess my life up by half measures when I can go the whole way? I spent the afternoon at Chester Meadows. I took some blue nylon rope with me and hung it from the old tree. I'd intended to hang myself with it, but when I put the noose round my neck I started to cry and couldn't stop. All these memories of when we were kids came rushing back to me, like when me and Adam and some other kids we used to play with built a tree house and formed the Red Hand Gang. Zara and Beth and all the other girls used to get really annoyed cos we wouldn't let them in, so they brought a Wendy house down to the copse and formed the Pink Hand Gang. We used to have brilliant summers when we were kids – every day we'd gulp down our breakfasts, race out of the house and cycle to the meadows on our bikes. We'd stay there all

day until it started to get dark and our mums came looking for us. There were loads of us who used to play down
there – I wonder what they're all doing now. Anyway,
obviously, cos I am sat here writing this now, I didn't do
anything stupid. I feel a bit embarrassed to admit this,
but I spent the afternoon swinging across the river and
shrieking my head off. I think it's the first time since the
beating that I actually forgot about it. I'm thinking about
trying to rebuild the tree house. I need somewhere that's
just my own where no one can get to me.

Friday 5 May 2000 – 2:22am

I've been busy designing my tree house, it's going to be
brilliant. If me and Mandy were still together it would be
a perfect place for us to go to be alone. Maybe she'll see
it one day. I'm really missing her at the moment, not the
sex, I'm not missing that, just the companionship, our
chats, the way she used to look at me. I wish she wasn't
seeing Darren, it's bugging me so much. I know what
he's like, he doesn't care about her like I do, he just
wants a trophy girlfriend. I'll try and catch her alone
tomorrow, maybe she'll listen if I write her a letter.
Maybe this will help.

Dear Mandy,

*I'm really sorry for the way I've been acting
lately. I know I've really upset you, but I've had a
lot on my mind. Just because we're not together
any more, it doesn't mean we can't be friends. I
know you think I don't deserve your friendship*

after the way I treated you, but you of all people
know how much it means for your friends to stick
by you when you're going through a rough patch.
I want to tell you about what's been going on,
but I can't in a letter.

Please meet me for a drink so we can talk.

Luke

I might as well go round to her and deliver this now
while I'm awake.

11:20pm

I woke up late this morning, and when I went downstairs
for some breakfast my letter to Mandy was on the door-
mat. She's scrubbed out her own name and put mine on
the front. She'd also written 'Not interested' on it. I went
round to her place but her mum said she wasn't there.
She looked at me differently to how she did the other
week, like she didn't like me or trust me any more. I'm
getting pretty used to those kinds of looks. I went round
to The Dog to see if she was with Darren and Mr O said
they were upstairs. I went up and walking in on them
snogging, it made me sick. They were both really hostile
and Darren tried to chuck me out. I begged Mandy to talk
to me but she wouldn't listen and Darren shut the door
in my face. If it wasn't for him, we'd be okay. I hate the
way he keeps coming between us and stopping me from
seeing Mandy. I tried to get back in, but he'd locked the
door. I was punching and kicking it, trying to get back in,
but Mr O came upstairs and threw me out – even he told
me to accept Mandy's moved on. I sat outside for a while,
trying to get my head together, I felt humiliated, I felt like
I'd made a fool of myself. Mandy and Darren left a few

minutes later. They didn't see me but I heard them talking. Mandy was saying I'm freaking her out and that she's scared of me. How could she be?

Tuesday 9 May 2000 – 10:43pm

I've been working on the tree house today. It's funny cos I hated carpentry at school, but this feels kind of therapeutic. I tried not to think about Mandy– it was hard though cos I just feel like it's not fair. She's got this warped impression of me that I've turned into a stalker and there's no way I can prove to her I'm not cos she won't talk to me. I went to The Dog at lunch time to apologize to Mr O. He tried to give me some fatherly advice but I wasn't in the mood for someone else thinking they know what's best for me. When I was leaving, I bumped into Mandy – she was with Cindy. I could see her physically clam up and look anxious as soon as she saw me, it makes me sad, I don't want this, this isn't how it's meant to be. I asked her if she had a few minutes, just so I could explain, but she did that horrid girly thing and said whatever I had to say I could say it in front of Cindy, so I gave up. When I came home this evening, Mum said we should have a chat. She said she doesn't know what's been going on, but she'd had a call from Mandy and I've got to leave her alone. I can't believe she went to Mum instead of coming to me. Does she hate me that much?

Friday 12 May 2000 – 3:41am

I had the dream again, but this time Darren was doing it to me and not Mandy. There's no way I'll get back to sleep now. I had the worst day yet yesterday. I'd started to miss playing football, so I went along to watch the game. I hadn't banked on Darren playing, apparently he's taken my place on the team. Mandy was there too – I know she thinks I'm following her, but I'm not. Gibbs was there. I thought I could handle it, but man was I wrong. First of all Mandy had a go at me and threatened to get the police involved if I don't leave her alone, then Darren came over and stuck his nose in, for a change. The worst part was that when Gibbs and his mates heard the commotion and saw I was there, they started on at me too. Luckily this time I wasn't frozen to the spot. As soon as I saw him coming over I legged it. I was sweating like mad, and I could hardly breathe. I just had to get out of there. They started yelling at me, that I'd only come to check out all the players in their shorts. All I could hear was them chanting loser, loser, loser as I ran away, like the chicken I am. The thing is they were right, I am a loser. I have no girlfriend and no life – what's the point in my even being here?

Sunday 14 May 2000 – 10:32pm

Mandy told me she wouldn't go back to me if I was the last man on earth today, she reckons I'm sick in the head. I don't understand why she hates me so much, I just want to be her friend, I need someone to talk to. This is never going to go away, is it? I had to work in Deva today and Darren came in to have a go at me. It was really embarrassing cos he was yelling all this stuff about me stalking Mandy in front of Adam. When Adam asked him what was going on he told him I'm a psycho and I won't leave Mandy alone. The only way to shut him up was to punch him and then we had a massive scrap, and some of the customers had to pull us apart.

10:40pm

Adam's just been in to give me some advice – he reckons I should get over Mandy cos she's not going to have me back and she's not worth losing my mate over. He told me to grow up cos I'm irritating and depressing the whole family, especially him.

11:12pm

Everyone thinks I'm mad, no one wants to know me any more. I hate myself. Everyone thinks I'm weird. I'm a loser, a sad, pathetic, miserable waste of space. I just want to get away from it, I don't want to spend the rest of my life feeling like this, dirty, seedy and ashamed. I can't stay here tonight, there's no point in prolonging the agony, I'm going back to Chester Meadows. I'll leave my diary on the screen, so they can find out why I'm doing this. I'm too ashamed to tell them.

Diary.doc

Dear Mum, Dad, Adam, Beth and Zara,

I'm so sorry for what I'm about to do.
Please forgive me.

I love you all.

Luke

PS Tell Mandy I never meant to upset her.

Wednesday 24 May 2000 – 11:40pm

Everyone knows about it, well, Adam, Mum and Dad. I didn't get to Chester Meadows cos I crashed the car on the way. I was crying so much I couldn't even see straight and then there was this massive bang and I can't remember after that. I woke up in hospital and was disappointed I wasn't dead.

Thursday 25 May 2000 – 4:23pm

Somehow the police have managed to work out I was trying to top myself and now no one will leave me alone. It's like being under constant surveillance.

Friday 26 May 2000 – 7:20pm

I told Adam about what happened and he's been great, really supportive. He told Mum and Dad for me cos I couldn't face it. Mum's really shocked, she's trying to act brave for me, but I hear her crying at night. Dad says he believes me, but he's lying. I think he thinks I'm gay, he doesn't know how to act around me, he looks awkward when it's just the two of us in a room. I can tell he's wondering how I could have let it happen.

Monday 29 May 2000 – 11:12pm

This is all getting out of hand, I wish I'd never told anyone. Adam went after Gibbs today and had a massive fight with him. He's denying everything. I know Adam's only looking out for me, but I wish he hadn't done that, cos now Gibbs is really going to have it in for me again. As well as all that, Zara's really upset cos some of the kids at school know about what happened to me and are giving her a hard time about it, calling us a psycho family and all that. She blames me for screwing up her life – excellent, just give me a chance to ruin Beth's too and I'll have a hat trick.

Tuesday 30 May 2000 – 6:01pm

Adam found me some stuff on male rape on the internet – he gave me this list of sites, too. Said I should make a note of them in case I wanted to find out more about them.

http://www.survivors.org.uk

http://www.aruk.co.uk

http://www.abny.demon.co.uk/acal

http://www.mrpp.org

He wants me to report Gibbs to the police. He reckons, seeing as I still have the clothes I was wearing the night it happened, they can be used as evidence. I know he's only trying to help but I don't even want to think about it. Dad is staying very quiet. I think he'd rather sweep it under the carpet and pretend it hasn't happened.

10:55pm

I heard Dad talking to Adam earlier. He was saying he can't get his head round what's happened and he wants him to find out if it wasn't just a game that went a bit too far. I knew people wouldn't believe me, but I thought at least Dad would try to. There's no way I'm going to the police now, no way.

Wednesday 31 May 2000 – 8:30pm

Mandy came round to see me today – she'd heard about the accident. She told me she feels really bad cos she didn't realize how bad things had got for me. She asked me to tell her what it was all about, but I've gone through it so many times with Adam, Mum and Dad over the past few days, I just couldn't face it. She was so nice to me. I'm glad she doesn't think I'm stalking her any more.

Thursday 1 June 2000 – 10:19pm

Adam's angry with me cos I burnt the evidence on the

149

barbecue last night. I don't care what he says, it's my life, my decision. There'd be no point me reporting Gibbs cos no one would believe me, it's just my word against his. I know there were two other people there, but they're his mates, they're not going to grass him up. Mandy came round again today and I told her everything. She's really upset about it, she feels really guilty cos of all the times she snubbed me when I tried to talk to her. I told her not to beat herself up about it, I'm just glad she understands. She thinks I should go to the police, too. She said they were brilliant with her. I'm sure they were, but it's different for girls.

Friday 2 June 2000 – 11:11pm

I had my first maths exam today. It was awful – I didn't know anything cos my head's been too cabbaged to study since you-know-what. I had a huge panic attack in the middle of it. I couldn't breathe, I just had to get out of there. Mum doesn't think I should even try and do my 'A' levels this year after what I've been through, but I feel like I have to. The way I'm feeling, if I don't do them now, I never will. There's no way I'm going through another year of school after this, I couldn't hack it.

Monday 12 June 2000 – 2:07am

Can't sleep. Mandy came round yesterday and we went for a walk to Chester Meadows, I showed her the tree house and she thought it was great. It's so good to finally have someone to talk to, I mean some of the things she says about how she felt after her dad raped her are uncanny. It's like, everything I'm feeling now, Mandy has already been there and she knows just what to say. I told her that the hardest part for me is the guilt – even though I know I didn't want it to happen and there was nothing I could have done to stop it, I still feel like it was my fault. I used to be so arrogant and cocksure. I know I provoked him when I slammed that car door on his leg. Mandy says she felt like that too, but you have to train your mind not to dwell on thoughts like that as they can really screw you up. Just having Mandy to talk to makes me feel so much more human again.

8:40pm

So much for all the progress I thought I was making. Gibbs came round here earlier. After all the talk of never letting anyone overpower me again, I couldn't even shut the door on him before he was inside the house. He reckons he was only having a laugh that night and I must have imagined him raping me cos he would never do anything that gross to another bloke. He leaned his face right into mine and said it didn't happen and he's got two witnesses. Luckily Adam walked in and he scarpered, I felt pretty shaken up for a while and I puked, but now I just feel angry. After everything he's done, how dare he come here and intimidate me. He obviously only came round cos he's scared this is all going to come out and go to court. He should be scared, cos I've decided to tell the police.

Wednesday 14 June 2000 – 5:45pm

Zara's in trouble again at school for bullying. I just had a massive go at her cos I know how it feels to be on the receiving end. I think she really thought about it cos I told her I bet the kids she bullies cry themselves to sleep and pretend they're ill so they don't have to go to school and face her. I don't think she'd ever thought about how what she does affects other people. I asked her what she'd do if one of the kids she bullies tried to top themselves like I did, and she went very quiet. Hopefully, she's having a good think about it.

Thursday 15 June 2000 – 8:32pm

I went to the police yesterday. It was really difficult cos even though I knew it was their job to take me seriously, I was sure they thought I was gay or I'm some kind of wimp to let this happen to me. None of the officers said anything – it was more the way they seemed uncomfortable around me, like they couldn't smile in case I took it as a come-on or something. Adam reckons I'm reading too much into everything, but Mandy understands the paranoia that starts to eat away at you. Having the medical was the second worst experience of my life, it was so degrading. The doctor was professional about it, but neither of us wanted to be there. I do want to get Mark back for what he did, but it's only today I've realized that I'm going to have to keep going over everything that's happened, telling loads of different people the same story in detail. It's hard to talk about something you're trying to forget. I met

Mandy afterwards and she gave me the number of her counsellor who's specially trained to help rape victims. I used to think that counselling was for crazy Americans with too much money, but I might look into it.

Friday 16 June 2000 – 2:12am

I can't sleep again, it's not the dreams that are keeping me awake, just the nightmare of what lies ahead. I had a talk with Dad today – he doesn't want me to take it to court. He didn't say it in so many words, but he was really trying to encourage me not to. He said I have to think about the possibility I might lose, and how everybody is going to find out about what happened. He's ashamed, I know he is. We were going to have some family counselling this morning, but when we got to the police station Gibbs was there. I just totally bottled it. Dad was mad with me. He says if this is going to go to court, then I'll have to face him. I know all that, I just couldn't hack it today.

9:45pm

I just got a call from DC Barnes – Gibbs has been charged with rape and assault.

Monday 19 June 2000 – 11:30pm

I haven't been able to sleep all weekend. It's been so hot and I just walk to Chester Meadows every night and sit in the tree house. It's better not being able to sleep out there, than being stuck in the house listening to Mum and William doing it. I feel trapped, like there's no going back on telling the police. I want Gibbs to be punished, I really do, but I'm not sure if I can go through with it. What if the case gets dismissed? What if I lose? Not only will I have to deal with the fact that no one believes me, but Gibbs'll come after me big time for reporting him. At least it won't be for a while, cos his application for bail was refused today.

Thursday 22 June 2000 – 11:18pm

It's in the paper today. It doesn't mention my name, but I'm sure everyone knows it's me. Dad said he heard Darren mouthing off about it. If he's worked it out, then the whole of Hollyoaks will know by tomorrow. Apparently he doesn't believe me and thinks I made it up cos I'm bent and I made a pass at Mark and he knocked me back. I don't know why I'm even bothering to try and take this to court, that's what everyone's going to think. Dad wants me to jack it all in, cos Gibbs' lawyers are going to really give me hell. He reckons they're going to try and make out I'm a liar and I wanted to have sex with him. Everyone thinks that already. I might as well go through with it, I've got nothing left to lose.

Monday 26 June 2000 – 11:12pm

Just had a visit from Darren, he's such a jerk, I can't believe I ever thought he was decent. He told me

Mandy's not coming to see me any more, cos she doesn't hang round with gay boys. He had a go at me for what I'm putting Gibbs through. I didn't realize they were so buddy-buddy these days. I hate knowing Mandy's with him. It's not cos I want her back cos too much has gone on for us to get together again. I just don't think he's right for her. I don't like who he hangs out with, they're dangerous.

Tuesday 27 June 2000 – 10:43pm

I'm knackered. I had my first counselling session today with a bloke called Simon. He's alright, I thought he'd be some incense-burning, beansprout eater, but he was dead normal – in fact we spent most of the hour talking about football. He says it's good I keep a diary cos it helps to sort your head out after something like this. He also said that most men who rape other men aren't gay themselves and it's nothing to do with sex, it's all about power and humiliation. I still don't get how anyone could do it. I told Simon about getting a stiffy when it was happening and how ashamed and sick I feel about it. I asked him if he thought that meant I was gay and he said it happens to loads of men, it's an involuntary reaction. I only had to tell him what I wanted to, which turned out to be everything. It was weird, just like this massive release, just talking to someone who knows exactly where you're coming from and isn't repulsed or horrified by it. Mandy's been great and she does understand, but she'll never totally get it cos she's not a bloke.

Friday 30 June 2000 – 9:06pm

Mandy came to see me yesterday, she's only just found out about Darren coming round. She's finished with him and I can't begin to describe how pleased I am about that. She's a really special girl and she wasted herself on him. If one good thing has come out of all this, I'm finding out who my real friends are. I haven't spoken to Jez for months.

Wednesday 5 July 2000 – 3:55am

I went to see Simon again yesterday and I went a bit mad. I just got so angry about the whole thing and I was ranting like a mad man. I feel better for it, but a bit embarrassed too. I keep having these fantasies about how I can get Gibbs back, I keep daydreaming about being in the courtroom and blowing him to oblivion with an Uzi and seeing his guts splattered all over the jury. Simon thinks I should have an HIV test, but I don't even want to think about it. I can't sleep.

Thursday 6 July 2000 – 8:34pm

I spent the rest of the night in the treehouse last night and was planning on staying there all day, but Mandy came and found me. I told her about what Simon said about the HIV test and she thinks I should definitely have one. I'm not sure though, isn't it better not to know about certain things? I mean, if I have got it, then I'm going to die anyway and I'd rather be taken by surprise than live every day expecting it to happen.

Friday 7 July 2000 – 8:21pm

I feel like I've got a bit of my life back. Mandy persuaded me to go for an HIV test in the end and she came with me. I haven't got it, but I can't help wishing Gibbs had it, that would be the best revenge, to watch him die a slow painful death.

Saturday 8 July 2000 – 11:43pm

I'm trying not to let Gibbs control my life any more and I've been working in Deva today. I had a few times when I got a bit psyched by it, like when Darren came in and had a go at me, but mostly it was okay.

Tuesday 11 July 2000 – 11:51pm

Not such a good day today cos Zara's started blaming me for kids at school having a go at her. As Dad said, the whole world seems to know, but if she thinks it's tough on her, then she should try being me. I do feel guilty for what I'm putting them all through but when I spoke to Simon today, he made me realize that the court case is necessary not only for justice, but so I can work through this whole thing and then move on.

Wednesday 12 July 2000 – 11:32pm

I feel pretty wound up – we find out tomorrow if my case can go to court. I wish I'd never burnt the clothes I was wearing that night. What if it gets thrown out for insufficient evidence? I'll have put myself and my family through all this and there won't be any resolution at the end of it. I told Mandy about the nightmares and she said it's just my mind processing the trauma of what happened, and they will ease and finally disappear. She's trying to encourage me, but I know she still gets them.

Thursday 13 July 2000 – 5:30pm

It's happening, it's been committed to the Crown Court and all three of them have had their bail refused. So this is it then, there's no turning back now.

Friday 21 July 2000 – 2:36pm

I'm on holiday in France with Mum and Beth. I needed to get away from all the gossip and speculation back home. Beth's already hooked up with some moped-riding smooth-talker and Mum's got William arriving tonight. I don't mind, though. It's not as if I haven't got stuff to think about. I change my mind a million times a day about whether or not I'm doing the right thing by taking Gibbs to court. The thought of telling all those people what happened and reliving that night time and time again terrifies me, but I know I have to face what happened if I want to get on with my life. I keep reminding myself that I have been humiliated, ridiculed and degraded once already and it can't be any worse than that. It isn't about winning or losing, it's about regaining my self-respect. If I don't get up there and tell the world what he has done, then I'll feel like I am accepting that it is okay for him to do that to me. And it's not okay, it's not okay for anyone to be raped.